When Christm

By Lucy

CW01513069

Prologue

Rosie Kilbride had just put her chocolate roulade into the oven when her mobile phone rang. She frowned. Who on Earth would be calling her this early? She fished the device from her rear jeans pocket and peered at the screen. Her frown deepened as she saw the name on the display, and she pressed the button to answer.

"Mum? What are you doing up at this time of the morning on a day off work? Is everything all right?"

"Hello, love." Victoria Kilbride's voice didn't sound quite right. It was croaky, almost strangled. "No, I'm afraid everything's *not* all right. Not at all. Your father and I have been up half the night with sore throats, runny noses, raging temperatures, coughing and spluttering. It's not a pretty sight. We're bloody miserable."

Rosie's heart sunk. It was obvious where this conversation was going. "Oh, Mum. I'm sorry to hear that. Is there anything I can do? Anything I can bring? I can go to the shop, or the chemist, if you need me to."

"Thank you, sweetheart, but given the time of year, the cupboards are packed to the gills with the usual remedies. And tissues. Thank God. At least my red nose is timely—I only hope I don't get called upon to head up the big man's sleigh tonight. I haven't got it in me."

Rosie couldn't help the smile that crept over her face. As well as her top-notch sense of humour—the presence of which showed there was nothing seriously wrong—her mother always did have a well-stocked medicine cabinet. There was no catching her out. "Okay, but what about food? I can whip up a few bits and pieces and bring them over to you to reheat. Save you cooking while you feel crap."

"Aww, that's a lovely offer, but I don't want to put you to any trouble."

"Don't be daft—it's no trouble. I'm already in the kitchen. I just put the roulade in the oven, ready for tomorrow. I'm guessing our plans have changed now, though."

There was a pause as her mother exploded into a coughing fit, by the sounds of it having moved the phone away from her face as she did so. After a moment, an even croakier-sounding Victoria came back on the line. "S…sorry, love. Bl…oody cough. It's awful." She cleared her throat, then drew in a sharp breath of discomfort. "And I feel like I've swallowed a packet of razor blades. Your dad's worse. His voice has all but disappeared."

"Well, you *did* say you wanted a quiet Christmas," Rosie quipped, hoping her silly joke might lift her mother's mood.

The response was a breathy laugh. "You're right, I did. But this wasn't exactly what I had in mind. I wouldn't wish this on my worst enemy, much less your dad. Or you, sweetheart. Maybe we can have a belated Christmas Day once the pair of us have cleared whatever this bug is? I'm so sorry. We were really looking forward to spending the day with you." She groaned. "Oh, and all that lovely food you've bought! Can any of it be salvaged, frozen or whatever?"

Pushing her disappointment down in the hopes it wouldn't come through in her voice, since she didn't want her mother to feel any guiltier than she clearly already did, Rosie replied, "Don't be silly, Mum, you've got nothing to apologise for. You didn't ask to get ill. I'll sort the food. Nothing will go to waste, I promise. How about I drop your presents off in the morning, along with a nice casserole? Something nice and tender, easy to eat, given your sore throats. And maybe some homemade soup."

"Just at the doorstep, love. We really don't want to pass this nasty virus or whatever it is on to you." She sighed. "I'm so pissed off and disappointed. Not only can we not spend the day with you, and enjoy your delicious cooking, you're now stuck spending the day on your own. I bet it's too late to make other arrangements, isn't it?"

"Oh, don't worry about that, Mum. A day by myself isn't going to kill me. I'll take advantage of the peace and quiet, after a mad few weeks at work. Have a rest."

"But it's *Christmas*."

As if she could forget, given her kitchen worktops and the fridge were packed full of festive accoutrements. Purely to appease her mother, with no actual intention of doing so, she crossed her fingers to negate the lie and said, "I'll send a few WhatsApps out, see if anyone's got room for a little one. You never know, someone might take pity on me. Especially if I offer to bring food."

"Yes, yes, good idea," Victoria replied, sounding brighter. "I'm sure someone can squeeze you in."

"I'm sure they can." Rosie rolled her eyes at the fibs tripping effortlessly off her tongue. They were only white lies, though, told to spare her mother's feelings, rather than being due to any malice.

"Right, well, I'd better let you go. Put your feet up, Mum. Dad, too. I'll crack on with making a couple of meals for you and drop them round in the morning with your presents, okay?"

"J—"

"Just at the doorstep, Mum, I know. I won't come in, I promise. I'll ring the bell, put the stuff down and step away from the plague-infested house, okay?" She was teasing, of course, but if she was honest, she *didn't* want to pick up whatever bug her parents were suffering with. It sounded awful—and she was due back to work on Boxing Day. The shop she owned and ran would be closed, but she planned to use the time to prepare the post-Christmas sale *and* return the shop to its pre-Christmas state. She couldn't afford any time off.

"Okay, sweetheart. Thank you. See you tomorrow."

"Bye. Love you. Feel better."

"Love you too. And sorry again. We're so disappointed."

"Don't give it another thought, Mum. I'm gutted, too, but these things happen."

"I know, but the timing couldn't be worse."

"Go and *rest*, Mum!"

"I'm going. Bye, love."

"Bye." Rosie hung up before her mother could continue lamenting their rotten luck, and stuffed her phone into her pocket. It *was* awful, and she *was* gutted, but spending ages on the phone grumbling about it wasn't going to change anything. Plus, despite her casual, placating words, most of the food she'd bought really needed to be cooked and eaten within a couple of days. And, since she had no intention of inserting herself, particularly so last minute, into any of her friends' festive plans, she needed an alternative. Her brother, James, was probably already enjoying his first Christmas in Australia with his wife and children, which was the reason hers and their parents' Christmas was going to be a quiet one. Before the move, they'd had several years of chaotic, child-centric festive periods. Thanks to their absence, this year was already going to be weird, without illness being thrown into the mix.

As she went to the fridge, wondering what else she could make for her parents, the much-needed alternative sprang to mind. She retrieved her phone once more, found the number she needed and tapped the button to dial.

"Hey, Ingrid. It's me. Do you still need volunteers for tomorrow?"

Chapter One

Christmas Day morning

Rosie forced a smile so wide at her parents through her car window she thought her face was going to crack. With a final wave, she pulled away from their house, where they stood huddled by the front door in their pyjamas, slippers and dressing gowns, feeling sorry for themselves, and headed for Ingrid's café. She felt terrible leaving them when they were so poorly—and on Christmas Day, too—but they'd insisted they'd be just fine, particularly thanks to the meals she'd brought with her, and had promised the three of them would have a re-do when they were feeling better. They had their presents to open, too, which would hopefully cheer them up a bit. Her own from them, now stashed safely in the boot of her car, would have to wait until she got home from the café later on that day. At least it gave her something to look forward to.

Satisfied she'd done everything she could to help her parents, she turned her attention to what lay in her immediate future. Rather than throwing herself on someone's mercy and blagging an invite to their place, or spending the day by herself, she was doing something *way* better.

Local café owner Ingrid, whom Rosie had got to know well and become very friendly with after attending the café both for the usual reason—food and drink—and some of the craft workshops hosted there, was a truly good egg. She'd been running a scheme for the past few years where she'd hosted a free Christmas meal for those who found themselves alone on the big day, or were unable to cook a Christmas dinner for themselves, whether for physical or financial reasons. It was funded by local donations, run by Ingrid herself, and staffed by fellow good eggs.

While Rosie had happily donated money to the cause before—and had even had a collection box in her own shop to help raise funds for it—she'd never been in a position to physically help out, since she'd always spent Christmas with her family. But, thanks to her cancelled plans, now she could. What a great way to make the best of a bad situation. Not only did she get to be useful, she wasn't spending the day by herself, *and* none of the food she'd bought would go to waste—she was bringing what she hadn't made into food parcels for her parents with her. Including what remained of the chocolate roulade—having left a generous portion each for her mum and dad, along with some mince pies and jam tarts. They certainly wouldn't starve.

She'd managed to bury her disappointment after speaking to her mother the previous morning by continuing to cook up a storm in her kitchen—both before and after work. As well as the roulade and the meals for her parents, she'd made more than enough mince pies and jam tarts for the patrons of the charity meal to eat one at lunch *and* take one home to have with their supper. She'd never wanted to do it on a professional basis, but baking had always been her go-to activity for stress relief and relaxation. The fact she'd see people enjoying the fruits of her labours—hopefully—was the icing on the cake.

As was usual for their part of middle England, there was no white Christmas. Just a sky full of gloomy grey clouds, which were letting loose a weak, persistent drizzle. *Preferable to pissing it down, I suppose.* She made her way into town, her mood lifting at the sight of the festive lights strung on the homes and businesses, the cheery decorations and *Santa Stop Here* signs stuck into people's front lawns and flowerbeds. Excitement would no doubt be reigning in those homes, as young children pounced on their piles of presents and began an unwrapping frenzy, while exhausted, bemused parents clutched mugs of strong coffee and watched on from the sidelines.

Of course, not everyone was so fortunate, which was why Ingrid's scheme was such a good one. A desperately needed one, in some cases. People ended up by themselves on Christmas Day for a multitude of reasons—she was a testament to that fact. Some might even prefer it. But for those who didn't, those who would cherish—possibly even be desperate for—the company as much as the food, today's event might well be the highlight of their festive season. The only bright spot in an otherwise dull, lonely few days.

She smiled. Her own Christmas plans might have gone tits up, but being even a tiny cog in a machine that would make a collection of deserving people happy was something to feel good about. She'd also been able to answer her mother's anxious question about where she was going truthfully: "To Ingrid's. She's already got a big group in, so one more wasn't a problem. Should be a damn good spread."

She'd scurried off then, hoping if her mother's virus-addled brain allowed her to actually remember what Ingrid had been doing on Christmas Day for the last few years—and she definitely knew, as she'd donated money each time—it'd be too late to pass comment.

Granted, she'd be helping to serve forty people their meals before getting so much as a crumb of a roast potato herself, but that was a small price to pay.

Conscious she was already a little behind schedule, thanks to her mother's wittering, she put her right foot down a smidgen harder. Soon, she pulled up outside the front door of the café. The town, unsurprisingly, was completely deserted, so she didn't worry about anyone complaining about her parking. It was only temporary, while she unloaded all her goodies. She gave a couple of light bips on her car horn before killing the engine, taking off her seatbelt and getting out of the vehicle. She closed the door, then zipped her coat and pulled up the hood against the cold and wet. By the time she was around at the boot, opening it to reveal tinfoil-covered trays and plastic containers galore, Ingrid appeared beside her, looking every inch the festive host, in her sparkling boots, glittery leggings, snowman-festooned knitted jumper, reindeer earrings, and headband with a sprig of mistletoe hanging off it.

"Morning," Ingrid said with a warm smile, before wrapping her in a hug. "Merry Christmas. I'm really sorry about your mum and dad not being well, but I'm definitely not sorry you're here. We were already stretched, and now one of my waitresses has phoned, saying she's poorly and can't come. So your extra pair of hands is very much needed—and appreciated."

She returned her friend's embrace, then let go and stepped back. "Merry Christmas, Ingrid. I'm glad to be here. Sorry I'm a bit late. I've just dropped some food parcels off at Mum and Dad's, along with their presents, so they're all set for a couple of days. Poor things are still feeling rough as anything. Food wise, whatever was left that I couldn't safely freeze, or was way too much for me to eat alone over the next few days, I brought. So there's a lovely joint of beef, potatoes, vegetables, a chocolate roulade, and a bunch of mince pies and jam tarts. The last three are homemade—not shop bought."

Ingrid narrowed her eyes. "You made chocolate roulade, mince pies *and* jam tarts? You surely didn't need all that just for the three of you? I know folks like to stuff their faces at Christmas, but come on…"

"All right, all right," Rosie said with a laugh, holding her hands up. "You got me. I'd already started on the roulade when I got the call from my parents to say they were ill, and was going to make a batch of mince pies, since they're my dad's favourite. But in the disappointment of having my plans derailed, I drowned my sorrows in baking. Happy now?"

Ingrid responded by reaching into the car boot and scooping up two big containers. She licked her lips exaggeratedly and wiggled her eyebrows. "Bloody ecstatic. I *love* mince pies." With that, she turned neatly on her heel and hurried inside.

Chuckling to herself, Rosie followed suit. The warm, cosy café was already a hive of activity with the tables being set, Christmas crackers added to each place setting, and people whizzing here, there and everywhere. The place had been decorated for the festive season to within an inch of its life since early December, but Rosie spotted at least a handful more decorations she didn't recognise from when she'd popped in a couple of weeks earlier to drop off hers and her customers' donations for the very meal she was now helping with—as well as treating herself to coffee and a slice of cake. She was normally a more regular patron, even if it was just a takeaway, but the run up to Christmas had been hectic in the shop, so she hadn't had the chance to pop in.

"Leave them there, hon," Ingrid said, pointing to the counter, where she'd already deposited the two boxes she'd carried in. "We'll get everything in pronto, so you can park your car, then I'll introduce you to everyone and get you all set up in your role for the day."

"No worries," she replied, setting her load down and following Ingrid back out the door to her car.

It wasn't long before she slammed her boot closed and gave Ingrid a wave as she slid into the driver's seat and drove to the car park at the end of the road. Her vehicle safely parked and securely locked, she hurried back to the café—picking up her pace and hunching deeper into her coat as the drizzle turned heavier.

She burst through the front door to the sound of Christmas music blaring out. Some of the other helpers were singing and dancing as they worked. It looked as though the party had already started—and the guests weren't even expected to show up for another couple of hours.

"Ah, there you are," Ingrid said, appearing from nowhere. "Let's get your coat and bag hung up out the back. I thought given you enjoy baking, you'd be particularly useful in the kitchen, if that's all right with you? Unless you'd prefer to be at front of house?"

"No, if you need me in the kitchen, I'm totally fine with that. Use me however you see fit."

Her belongings stowed, and her own funky headband—a tiny, jaunty elf hat with an even tinier jingle bell affixed to its pointy end—settled in place, she straightened her oversized jumper, a knitted affair with gingerbread men and candy canes all over it, as she followed Ingrid. After being introduced to the wait staff she didn't know—the others worked in the café normally, so they were already acquainted—she and Ingrid made their way towards the kitchen.

Ingrid pushed open the 'in' door to reveal a bunch of people already working hard, despite the fact there weren't yet any diners. The clatter of trays, the rhythmic tapping of vegetables being chopped, and the whir of food processors filled the air—as did intense heat and the delicious scent of roasting meat.

"I've left the organisation in here entirely to my head chef for the day, since he knows what he's doing. He's the best there is. He works in some fancy place in the city, but somehow managed to wangle today off to help us out. Let's go and introduce you, and he can decide where he needs you the most, okay?"

Rosie nodded, then tailed Ingrid as she made a bee-line for a man in a white chef's jacket, and black and white checkered trousers. Rather than the tall, white hat one would usually expect a head chef to be wearing, he had on a Santa hat. He was tall, dark-haired, and had his broad back to them as he worked away at something on one of the stainless-steel surfaces.

"Hey, Chef," Ingrid said as they drew close, "got your last pair of hands here. She's good in the kitchen and ready to work."

The man stopped what he was doing, wiped his hands on a

tea towel and turned to them with a smile, which quickly faded as recognition kicked in.

"Rosie," Ingrid said, indicating her head chef, "this is—"

"Luke Adams," she interrupted, staring in disbelief at the man who'd broken her heart into a million pieces a decade ago. The very same heart which was now skipping like a rabbit on speed and sending heat rushing into her cheeks. *Fuuuuck. Merry fucking Christmas to me.*

Chapter Two

The heat of Ingrid's stare bored a hole into the side of Rosie's face. As if she wasn't hot enough. "You two... know each other?"

Oh, Christ. You could say that. She snatched in a sharp breath through her nostrils, which only made things worse as she caught the slightest whiff of Luke's cologne—his favourite and the one he'd worn while they were together. She gritted her teeth against the onslaught of memories threatening to pile into her head. Then, with a gargantuan effort, she settled her face into another one of those forced grins and turned to her friend, whose expression was a mixture of concern and intrigue. Hopefully the redness in her face would be put down to the heat from the kitchen, rather than the tumultuous state of her emotions.

"Oh, yeah," she wafted what she hoped looked like a dismissive hand and kept her tone as casual as she could manage, "known each other for yeeears, haven't we, Luke?" She shifted her gaze onto his face—a decade older, etched with a few more fine lines, but damn it, as handsome as ever. *Looking good at forty-two, Luke, you absolute bastard. Why couldn't you do the decent thing and resemble a bag of shit?*

Regardless of his appearance, she couldn't wrap her head around him being there. She'd had no idea he was even in the country, much less that he was working in a restaurant in their nearest city, a few miles away. Presumably he was living locally again, too.

How was it even possible he was back—and without her knowing? Their hometown was small, and as a local business owner, she was incredibly well connected, so how had the news of his return never reached her on the grapevine? Maybe the event that had rocked her world had been so irrelevant to everyone else it didn't occur to anyone to tell her. It *had* been a long time ago, after all. She hadn't even *been* a local business owner at that point.

"Yeah…" he said absently, taking a beat longer than her to recover. He gave a little shake of his head and switched on a megawatt smile, while his gaze flicked briefly up to her elf hat, down to her jumper, then back to her face. "How the devil are you, Rosie? Merry Christmas!"

"Merry Christmas! I'm good, thanks. Really good. How are you?" *Overexaggeration, much?*

"Right." Ingrid backed away, peering warily between the two of them through narrowed eyes, her brow creased. "There's loads still to do out front, so I'll leave you to make the introductions, Luke, if you don't mind. You know where I am if you need anything."

"Sure do," Luke said. "Thanks, Ingrid."

As soon as the door leading out of the kitchen swung shut, Rosie wheeled around to face Luke. She spoke quietly, not wanting the others to hear. "What the *hell* are you doing here? I thought you were in New York."

He cast a glance around, presumably to make sure no one else was paying them any attention, then focused on her. "I was. But now I'm not. Obviously." He groaned. "Look, it's a long story, but we don't have time for it right now. There's way too much to do.

Can we just get through today, and talk later?"

The heartbroken young adult still buried deep inside her wanted to tell him to shove his talk where the sun didn't shine, but the thirty-two-year-old woman who'd done a hell of a lot of growing up since then nodded. "Of course. We're adults. I'm sure we can work together for a few hours with no issues." She cleared her throat, hoping her next words didn't choke her. "So, you're in charge. Could you let me know where to find an apron, then give me a quick rundown of what's going on and what you'd like me to do, please?"

He assessed her face for what could only have been milliseconds, but felt like days, then gave a curt nod. "You still like baking?"

Ignoring the pang in her gut at him remembering that nugget of information, she replied, "I do."

"Great. Because I have a spot open in desserts. Let's find you that apron and get you set up."

He strode away, his long legs eating up the distance and leaving her to scurry behind him like a small child, while shooting daggers at his broad, still-muscular back. *Ugh. If I'd known he was here, I'd definitely have asked to work out front. Bloody hell. What convoluted series of events have taken place to put the two of us in the same room, at the same time, after all these years? Especially on Christmas sodding Day. I must have somehow got onto Santa's seriously-bloody-naughty list for this to be my present. A lump of coal would have been preferable.*

She breathed deeply and squeezed her hands into fists. She

couldn't fall apart, not now. Nor could she turn tail and run. There were forty people coming for their dinner soon, and from the limited amount she knew about commercial kitchens, they were a finely-tuned machine. If one thing went wrong, it could cause everything to grind to a halt. She was determined not to be that thing. She wanted to help, not hinder. And she definitely didn't want to give Luke a reason to look down on her. She needed to come across as the calm, capable, efficient woman she was when *not* faced with one hell of a blast from her past.

Rosie almost crashed into said blast from the past when he stopped without warning. She leapt back as he spun to face her, an apron bearing the café's branding dangling from his long fingers. *Huh. No wedding ring. Interesting. But then, would he wear it while he's at work?* "Here you are."

She tore her gaze from his left hand and took the apron with a mumbled, "Thanks." Then she relished the opportunity to stare at the floor as she slipped the strap over her head—not the easiest thing to do, as in her flustered state she'd forgotten she was wearing a novelty headband, which jingled madly as the strap got caught on it—and fumbled with the ties, before finally getting the thing secured around her waist.

Luke remained silent until she got herself sorted and looked up at him. Something swirled in those familiar hazel eyes—probably relief he'd got shot of her when he did—but quickly disappeared. "Okay." He clapped his hands and snapped into professional mode, before giving her a run through of the layout of the kitchen and all the food, equipment and people within it.

It soon became apparent her role meant she wouldn't have much to do with him at all for the majority of the shift—thank God. While each of the staff would jump in to help another person if needed, they'd mostly stick to their own areas. Luke would muck in with plating up courses and casting his eye over them before they went to the pass, meaning she had two whole courses to go before he would be hanging around in her part of the kitchen. As well as doing what she was here to do, she planned to use the time to get her shit together. When he finally reached her, she'd have been transformed into the coolest of cucumbers.

Once introductions were done, he led her to the area she'd be working in, reeled off a bunch of information, then jammed his hands on his hips and gave her a raised-eyebrow look. "Well, I think that's everything. Does that all make sense? Any questions? Concerns?"

She shook her head. "No, I'm all good, thanks. *Chef.*" She added the commonly-used mark of respect and hierarchy in a kitchen with a sickly-sweet smile. She was willing to pull up her big girl pants and work with the man, but that didn't mean she had to be *entirely* on her best behaviour, did it? As long as no one else noticed, it couldn't hurt. And it might just make getting through the day a little easier.

He gave her a dark look, the menacing effect of which was only slightly diluted by the scarlet Santa hat with its white fluffy trim still perched atop his head. "Brat," he murmured. Then one side of his lips tweaked up the tiniest bit, and a glint appeared in his eyes, making him look positively devilish. He leaned towards her, making her heart rate pick up. "There was a time when I'd have had you over my knee for that sort of behaviour."

Then he straightened, turned, and marched away, leaving her gaping after him, wondering whether the hubbub in the busy kitchen could possibly have caused her to mishear him.

But then, as he reached the sink beside his workstation, he glanced over his shoulder and gave her the biggest, most salacious wink she'd ever seen, before turning to wash his hands.

Rosie gulped, spun to face her own work area, and gripped the edge of the stainless-steel surface until her knuckles went white. *Nope, I didn't mishear him. He really did just make reference to spanking me. Something he's done on many, many occasions.*

She'd been so devastated when they split—or, more accurately, when he'd ditched her to take up a job offer on the other side of the Atlantic—that she'd reacted by throwing herself wholeheartedly into her career, her hobbies, and socialising, not allowing herself time to even think about him, much less miss him or mourn the loss of their relationship and a potential future together.

Now, though, looking back through the prism of time, she found herself thinking not of their break up, but of what had gone before it. Two years of fun, love, laughter and lots of smoking hot, BDSM-laden sex, with him firmly in control—of the latter, at least. In every other part of their relationship she'd been his equal, but in the bedroom happily and blissfully submissive.

Things had been so good between them, in fact, that when he'd suggested cooking a special dinner for her at his house one Saturday night, she'd been convinced he was planning to propose.

Her mind had raced, immediately running through potential locations and outfits and honeymoons, before hopping ahead to consider how many children they might have, and what they'd look like. At twenty-two, she hadn't been ready for the having babies part yet, but definitely wanted them in the future, and couldn't see herself having them with anyone other than Luke—whom she'd just known would be an amazing dad. He'd been fantastic with his younger cousins and his friends' kids, and would undoubtedly be even better with his own. *Their* own.

However, the bubble of their bright future had been unceremoniously popped when, after three delicious courses and a couple of glasses of wine, rather than producing a small velvet jewellery box and getting down on one knee, he'd dropped the bombshell that he'd be moving to New York. He'd been offered the opportunity of a lifetime at a brand-new restaurant, funded by disgustingly wealthy Wall Street types, and was being given carte blanche on the menu and staffing. The salary was insane, too.

Her visions of their fairytale wedding, luxurious honeymoon, and imagined cherubic children had disappeared in the blink of an eye. As had any hopes of a future with Luke Adams.

A particularly loud clang snapped her back to the present— and not a moment too soon. Despite being determined not to fall apart, she'd come dangerously close. Hardly surprising, though, given Luke's smutty, nostalgia-inducing comment, followed by that *wink*. Why did he still have to be so damn sexy? He looked great— even in his daft hat. Smelled great. It wasn't fair.

She shook her head, gripped the worksurface more tightly

still, until the discomfort in her fingers helped her to reboot her brain and bring everything into sharp focus. That done, she relaxed her hands, took a deep breath and reached for the sherry trifle recipe in front of her. Time to let baking relieve her stress, relax her, as it usually did.

But then, she didn't *usually* bake while in the same room as the ex-boyfriend who'd broken her heart a decade ago, did she?

Chapter Three

Thankfully, the requirement to concentrate on something other than her own inner turmoil got her through the next couple of hours. She kept her head down and did her best to steer clear of the playful banter being tossed around—not wanting to inadvertently get caught up in something that would give away her current emotional state or her feelings towards Luke. Not that she was entirely sure what those were yet.

As time ticked on, though, the atmosphere in the kitchen altered as the gear switched from prepping to actually getting ready to serve the meals. The banter disappeared, to be replaced by brief questions, commands, statements. The heat was on—literally *and* figuratively.

Despite the chaos in her brain, it was genuinely fascinating to see Luke in his natural habitat, playing to his skillset, honed through years of practice. She had no idea how well he knew the other kitchen staff, but he was clearly well liked, and thoroughly respected. She'd never admit it to anyone, not even under pain of death, but she was impressed. No wonder he'd gone far in his chosen career. *More than can be said for me.*

She pushed the unbidden thought aside and paid attention to what was happening around her. Given she was dealing with desserts, there was no major rush on her end at the moment, but it was entirely possible she'd be asked to help out elsewhere, depending on what was needed at any one time. The diners had been asked to arrive between twelve and half past, with a view to starting service at one. A glance at the wall clock revealed it to be ten past twelve.

Just then, Ingrid burst in, a look of mild panic on her face. "How's it going, everyone? Everything on track? Just to let you know, folks are arriving. They're certainly eager! We've got maybe a third of the expected numbers seated already."

"All good," Luke replied evenly, seeming as calm as Ingrid was the opposite. "Any changes to the plan? Surprises?"

During his intro, Luke had told Rosie the menu for the day had been kept as simple as possible. None of the staff were being paid to help out, so it seemed unfair to ask them to work with anything complicated or particularly time-consuming. Yes, they wanted to give people a wonderful lunch, but they also wanted to get away afterwards with enough time to have a relaxing evening with their own friends and families, too.

Starters consisted of prawn cocktail or pâté, with a mushroom pâté for vegetarians. Main was a full roast dinner, with a couple of options for meat, plus a nut roast for the veggies. Desserts were Christmas pudding, sherry trifle, or cheese and biscuits, as well as Rosie's last-minute additions of chocolate roulade, mince pies and jam tarts. The guests had been asked to let the kitchen know what they wanted in advance, so they could plan and prepare, but years of experience had clearly taught Luke things didn't always go to plan—hence his query.

"Not so far," Ingrid said, shaking her head, which made the mistletoe on her headband bob and wave wildly. Rosie suppressed a grin. "But I'll let you know if that changes. Hopefully not. I'll get the table orders in to you pronto. When starters are done and dusted, we'll be letting folks know there's also a little bit of beef available, in addition to the turkey and gammon." She smiled and nodded in Rosie's direction. "Then when mains are cleared away, we'll also offer the roulade, mince pies and jam tarts, with the option to let them take the latter two away with them for supper if they wish. Then we'll see what's left for us poor buggers, if anything. If this lot are as hungry as they are eager, it might just be crumbs!"

With a chuckle, she swept over to the pot-washing station, collected a tray of clean glasses and bustled back out front.

Luke clapped twice, loudly, gaining everyone's attention. "Okay, folks. You've done brilliantly so far, but now it's time to take things up another notch. But no need to stress. We're prepped, we know what we're doing, and no meal changes so far. Ten tables of four, served table by table. Rinse and repeat, twice. Calm, methodical, organised. Everyone ready?"

"Yes, Chef!" came the call from all sides—including Rosie, who wasn't being sarcastic or sassy this time. She was in this now, fully invested. She'd offered to help out today because she wanted to. Giving these people the best possible Christmas lunch was all that mattered—regardless of who was running the kitchen and what he'd once meant to her.

"Good." Luke turned to Hattie, who was dealing with the starters. "Okay, you're almost up. As long as there are no last-minute changes, we know the numbers. We're just waiting on what's required for each table." He glanced behind her to a huge, glass-fronted refrigerator, which was loaded with what Rosie assumed was the relevant number of prawn cocktails, ready to have the finishing touches placed on them, and nodded. "Right, good stuff. Soon as we get that info from Ingrid, I'll be back with you and we'll get those starters onto the pass, okay?"

Hattie bobbed her head, then returned her attention to where she'd been slicing up a delicious-looking loaf of brown bread, ready to be toasted and added to the plates of pâté.

Luke lifted the rim of his Santa hat and swiped his forearm over his brow, then settled the hat back into position before making short work of checking on the joints of meat, roasting potatoes and pigs in blankets. Seemingly satisfied with how things were progressing, he checked in with Mac. "All coming along here, mate?"

"Yes, Chef. All on schedule. Veggies, mash, stuffing and Yorkshire puddings will be ready when you are."

"Brilliant. You know the drill. Things will ramp up as soon as that last starter goes out the door." He clapped Mac on the back, and before Rosie knew which way was up, Luke was heading in her direction, his lips stretched into a wide smile.

"Last, but not least, Rosie! A baptism by fire for you. How are you getting on?"

She returned his smile, hoping it looked more confident than she felt. Though it was his presence, rather than any concern there were issues with her work knocking her for six. "On schedule, I reckon, Chef. By the time desserts are due to go out, I'll have everything prepped. Then the dishes will just need putting together when we know what's going where."

Luke cast a critical eye over her workstation, making her gulp. *So much for not being worried about my work. Oh God, please don't say I've fucked something up. I'm perfectly fine in the kitchen at home, when I'm cooking for friends and family. This commercial malarkey is all new to me. As is having a big-shot chef checking what I'm doing.*

He peered at her, lips pursed and one eyebrow cocked. "Looking good. Well done. Similar to what I just told Mac, things will really get going for you the second that last main meal goes out the door. Maybe before, depending on how quickly folks eat." He paused, then said more quietly, "Everyone else has done this before, and as far as I know, you haven't. So when I say shout up if you need any help, I mean it, okay? Every single person in this room will happily muck in if you need it—including me. *Please* don't let pride get in the way."

She'd barely opened her mouth to protest that she wasn't in the habit of letting pride get in the way of anything, when Ingrid hurried back in, waving slips of paper. Her headband had slipped a little now, making her sprig of mistletoe appear drunk. This time, Rosie couldn't help the amused snort that slipped out. Fortunately, nobody heard her as Ingrid trilled, "Two tables with drinks at their elbows, ready to eat whenever you're ready to feed them."

It wasn't quite half past twelve, let alone the one o'clock service they'd been aiming for, but Rosie guessed they wouldn't stand on ceremony, not when the food was all but ready to go. After all, the kitchen's collective stress level would decrease with each successfully served plate, so the sooner it began, the better. Maybe it'd even mean they could all get home that bit earlier.

"Fab." Luke took the slips of paper from Ingrid and eyed them as he moved over to his workstation. "Thanks. Coming right up."

"Great. Oh, and Luke?"

"Hmm?"

"Your dad says hello."

He paused in the act of attaching the paper slips to his order board, then let out a breath and smiled, his shoulders seeming to relax just a tad. "Oh, he's here already? I haven't had a moment to peek through the door and check. Tell him I said hello and I'll pop out as soon as I get a second, please."

"Will do."

As Ingrid passed through the 'out' door, one of the waitresses appeared through the 'in' door and hurried over to Luke with a note in her hand. "Here you go, another table ready for their starters."

"Great, thanks. Coming right up." He added the third slip to his board, then said, "Okay, Hattie, listen up." He reeled off the orders for the first and second tables, then immediately jumped in to help her. The pair of them moved swiftly, efficiently, murmuring to each other the whole time, presumably to make sure they were on the same page. Slices of toast and dollops of homemade chutney were added to plates of pâté, bread was placed on side plates to go with the prawn cocktails, and before Rosie's brain could catch up with what was happening, Luke had scrutinised each dish in turn, placed it on the pass and slammed his hand onto a bell before calling, "Service, please, table one!"

He moved over and yanked a slip of paper from his board, jammed it onto a metal spike, then turned back and began assisting Hattie with the second table. Two wait staff bustled in and whisked away the waiting orders.

Rosie shifted her attention to her own tasks, but kept half an eye on proceedings as she did so. The next little while was a constant flurry of perfectly choreographed activity: finish order, place on pass, summon wait staff, jam paper onto spike, wait staff collect food, finish next order, and so on. No near misses, no fuck ups, no fuss. Just a triumph of culinary creation. Even a couple of tweaks in menu choices didn't cause so much as a batted eyelid.

It was truly fascinating to see what happened behind the scenes in a commercial kitchen, and had already increased her appreciation of what they went through in order to feed large numbers of people in a timely fashion.

"Okay," she heard Luke say to Hattie, "you can handle the last table by yourself, right? I'm going to nip out and say hello to my dad. I won't be long—but come and get me if you need me." Then, "Mac, you're almost up. While I'm out there, could you do another check, make sure everything's okay? Meat, too?"

"Yes, Chef," came the reply.

Rosie glanced up to see Luke crossing the kitchen. Just before he drew level with her, he looked in her direction, an inscrutable expression on his face. He kept his gaze on her for as long as he could without having to turn his head, then he was gone, pushing through the 'out' door—the swinging of which allowed in the punctuated sounds of merriment from the main body of the café.

Chatting, laughter, the clink of cutlery, crockery and glasses, the bangs from crackers and party poppers, the dulcet tones of Noddy Holder and co singing *Merry Xmas Everybody*.

Having turned to watch him go, she snapped her head back around, hoping nobody had noticed. She didn't want anyone to think she was gazing after him like a lovesick teenager, when what she'd actually been doing was wondering why the hell he'd been staring at *her*.

She sighed and continued slicing cheese, ready for the cheese and biscuits. As far as she was concerned, this day couldn't be over soon enough. While she was happy to be doing a good deed, it was hard not to feel like she was actually being punished for it. At least if she'd stayed at home alone, she wouldn't have come face to face with her very own ghost of Christmas past.

Bah, humbug indeed.

She couldn't help wondering why Luke's dad was here, either. Where was his mum? Had they split up? Although she'd got along really well with the two of them, she hadn't had any contact with Luke's parents since their break up. A lot could happen in that time. Had the *worst* happened? She gulped. *God, I hope not.*

Chapter Four

True to his word, Luke wasn't gone long, and soon after he returned, the wait staff began whizzing into the kitchen with finished plates. Hattie, now helping with the pot-washing, grinned widely as one of the waitresses showed her the empty plates before putting them down on the pile of pots to be washed. "Good to see," she said. "Everyone enjoying themselves?"

"Definitely," the waitress replied, nodding so emphatically she almost unseated her reindeer antler headband. "Everyone seems to be getting on, making friends. I just found out two of them—a man and a woman in their eighties—who met at the lunch last year got on *so* well they got married at Easter!"

"*Easter*?" Rosie blurted out. "Blimey, that's quick, isn't it?" Despite her surprise, she also had a thought: if the newlyweds, despite not being on their own, lonely or whatever anymore, had still been allowed to come to the lunch, perhaps there was a less devastating reason Luke's dad was here.

The waitress shrugged. "Not when you're their age, it isn't." She made a soppy face and clasped her hands together in front of her chest. "I think it's lovely. Both widowed, resigned to being on their own for the rest of their lives, and then they find each other and have a second chance at happiness. Aww. Adorable. Anyway, must dash!"

As the waitress left, Ingrid came in clutching what Rosie assumed were the first bunch of main course orders. "No deviations from the plan, here—though two would very much like a slice of beef if it's going spare." Her mistletoe headband was nowhere to be seen this time. Had it tumbled off? Or had she removed it after receiving too many requests to pucker up from randy, single pensioners? She was an attractive woman—one could hardly blame them for trying, if that was the case.

"Excellent," Luke said, taking the slips from her and putting them on his board. "Thanks." He jerked his head towards the pot-washing station. "We just had word the starters are going down a treat. They certainly seemed to be when I was out there chatting to Dad, too."

Ingrid nodded. "They sure are. Though, it has to be said, so is the booze." She chuckled. "I'm deliberately slowing down drinks service and giving smaller measures until they've all had a bit more in their bellies to soak it up. I don't want to spend my afternoon pouring pissed people into taxis."

"Try saying *that* six times fast." Luke grinned. "Well, there's plenty of food to go around, so more than enough to take care of the soaking up. Let's get this lot fed until they're fit to burst. I'm going to start carving the meat in a second. Mains will be on their way within ten minutes."

"Thanks. You're a star." She placed her hand on his arm, then squeezed it, before addressing the room. "In fact, you're all stars. Seriously, everyone, I can't thank you enough for what you're doing today. I know you're stuck in here grafting and not seeing your work appreciated, but I assure you it is. A thousand percent. Those folks are having a wonderful time. Smiles and laughter all round. You should be very proud. I know I am."

She dashed off again, but not before Rosie spotted the glistening in her eyes. *Bless. This really means a lot to her.*

A glance at Luke revealed him to be staring after Ingrid, his own expression troubled. Rosie couldn't work it out. He'd been grinning at Ingrid seconds ago, but now he looked as though all the mirth had been sucked out of him. *Oh God, is it because his dad is here? More accurately, because of the* reason *his dad is here? And there was all that talk of being widowed, too. Maybe something bad has* happened to his mum. She felt sick to the stomach at the mere idea of it and, although it wasn't exactly a happy thought, found herself hoping like hell Luke's parents had merely divorced—it was vastly preferable to the alternative.

She took a deep breath and tried to focus on positive things, like the clear appreciation from Ingrid and the diners, rather than her darker, more depressing thoughts. It wasn't easy, though, and the sense of dread continued to clutch at her guts as she began removing the mince pies and jam tarts from their respective Tupperware containers and plating them up. She was almost done with her prep—all she could do then was wait until the dessert orders were confirmed before jumping onto the finishing touches, since it looked as though everyone else had their tasks handled.

More heat pumped into the already boiling kitchen as Luke began removing joints of meat from the oven and carving them, while Mac started grabbing the other items and sticking them under hot plates. Clanking and the roar of the electric carving knife joined the general cacophony of noise. Unfortunately, so did the luscious scents of the cooked food, and Rosie bit her lip as her stomach rumbled.

Suddenly, her hastily-scoffed bowl of cereal at breakfast felt like a really long time ago. She guessed when doing this job for a living, one got used to the sights and scents, became immune to them. She, on the other hand, was in severe danger of drooling onto the grapes. Unable to resist, and sure no one was looking, she popped a couple in her mouth, hoping they'd appease her growling tummy for a while.

With the meat carved and ready to be dished up, Luke checked the order slips and began calling out, and the finely-tuned routine began again—only this time on a bigger, more complex scale. Meat, potatoes, pigs in blankets, stuffing, Yorkshire puddings, vegetables. Jugs of gravy, cranberry sauce, apple sauce. It was even more of a dance than last time, and Rosie, with very little left to do until her orders came up, allowed herself a couple of minutes to just watch.

It was a truly amazing sight. All food establishment customers ever really saw were the finished meals, brought out by calm, efficient wait staff. They didn't see the perspiration-slick, red-faced chefs and pot-washers, the darting around, the intense concentration, the way all of the different sections of the kitchen worked together so seamlessly to provide a perfect dining experience.

Luke tinged the bell and called for service, barely pausing for breath before proceeding to read out the next lot of orders.

She peered through the porthole in the 'out' door to see a scene which went a little way towards chasing away some of the chill that had been caused by maudlin thoughts of what might have become of Luke's mum. As Ingrid and the wait staff buzzed around clearing plates and getting drinks, the paper-hat-wearing diners were all smiles and chatter, some even having a bit of a singalong to the music, which Rosie picked up when one of the waiters blasted through the 'in' door with armfuls of used crockery—Elton John's *Step Into Christmas.* Another waiter followed right behind him, and dashed over to collect some plates from the pass.

She grinned and hummed along to the upbeat tune, before catching sight of Luke's dad, John. He was well ensconced in the festivities, a bright-yellow paper hat atop his head, and wearing a knitted jumper featuring a grinning snowman. He was a good few years younger than the three other diners he was sharing a table with, but seemed to be having a fabulous time nonetheless. She wondered what had come first: John's attendance of this event, or Luke's involvement in it. Frowning, she figured she'd find out later on, if Luke still wanted to talk. She hadn't technically agreed to it, but now it seemed like it would probably be a good idea. Apparently, they had a lot to catch up on.

"'Scuse us, please," said the waiter who'd dropped off the dirty plates.

"Oh." Rosie, belatedly realising she was blocking the exit, leapt out of the way. "Sorry." The waiter hustled out, quickly followed by the one laden with delicious-looking Christmas dinners.

Tutting and shaking her head at her own stupidity, she spun back to her workstation and began double checking she'd done everything she needed to. Things were moving apace, and she didn't want to get caught out when it was her time to shine. Thankfully, it appeared she'd done a good job, so much so she literally didn't have a thing left to do until the dessert orders were called up.

"Hey, Rosie," Luke called, "can I borrow you a minute?"

Ignoring her skipping pulse—there wasn't time for that silliness right now—she nodded and hurried over. "Of course. What can I do?"

He pointed with his chin to some empty plates set off to one side. "We've got two vegetarian meals going out. Can you plate them up, please? They've got the nut roast. Vegetable wise, everything's the same, but obviously there are no pigs in blankets, and their roast potatoes have been cooked separately, as the main ones are done in goose fat." He grabbed one of the slips of paper, tore it carefully and handed one of the scraps to her. "Here you go— these are the exact requirements. Mac will show you where to find the nut roast and the separate potatoes. That okay?"

"Yes, no problem." She flashed him a bright smile, while internally panicking. Plating up main meals was way more complicated than desserts. There were so many more options. Still, she only had two to deal with, and she literally had the individual items written down, rather than having to remember them as Luke called them out, like he was the rest. All she had to do was carefully but quickly get everything on the list onto the two plates. *And* make it look nice.

Get a grip, woman! You're acting like you've never plated up a roast dinner before.

Gritting her teeth, she stuffed the slip of paper into her apron pocket, grabbed the two plates and sidled up to Mac. His face was set into a grim mask of concentration, and she really didn't want to interrupt him, but didn't have a choice. "Hi, Mac. Sorry to disturb you, but Luke's asked me to sort two vegetarian meals. Could you let me know where I'd find the nut roast and the vegetarian roast potatoes, please?"

He blinked, then looked at her with a distracted smile. He set down the large silver spoon he'd been using to ladle peas onto a plate and said, "'Course. Come with me." He moved to the far end of the work area, where a handful more spaces for hot plates sat. Only two were occupied. He grabbed a clean, sharp knife and serving fork, then speared the nut roast, lifted it onto the worksurface and began slicing it. "Five veggie meals in total. While there are more of the goose fat roast potatoes to come out of the oven, this is all we've got for the vegetarians, so just watch your portions, okay? We don't want the last person to be served to go without." He left two slices of nut roast out, but carefully replaced the other three in the hot plate to keep warm until they were needed.

"No problem. Thanks." Mac whizzed away to continue with his own task, while she set about hers. The first bit was easy; one portion of nut roast on each plate. Then she grabbed the spoon from the roast potatoes, snatching in a breath through her teeth as her hand contacted the hot metal, and began a rough count. Despite the fact they hadn't been cooked in goose fat, the potatoes still looked golden brown and crispy, and smelled divine. Her stomach gave another grumble of protest. She mentally crossed her fingers there'd be plenty of food left over so she and the other volunteers could have a nice meal, too. She doubted she'd have the energy to cook anything when she got home, so if not, her dinner would consist solely of snack foods.

After a little bit of mental arithmetic—then a little bit more, since it wasn't her strong suit and she wanted to ensure she'd got it right—she scooped up five potatoes onto each plate, replaced the spoon, then scurried back to where the rest of the hot plates sat. She settled her plates down on the worksurface and retrieved the order slip from her pocket. Typically, both diners wanted completely different things, so she decided to do one at a time. It possibly wasn't the most efficient way, but it *was* the only way she could be confident she wouldn't screw it up. She didn't want to be responsible for ruining anyone's Christmas dinner.

She dipped in and out of the various hot plates, dancing around Mac as he did the same, and finished her first order. Unsure what to do now, she approached Luke and held the plate out to him. "Er, vegetarian option, no peas?"

He paused in his task of dishing out thick slices of turkey, gammon and beef, gave her a warm smile and eased the plate from her grasp. She pressed her lips together to stifle a gasp as their skin contacted, sending a zing of awareness through her.

"Don't look so worried," he said softly, then peered down at the plate, made a couple of little tweaks, and put it on the pass. "You're doing fine. Where's the other one?"

"Coming right up, Chef. Two ticks."

"Great, thanks."

Clutching the scrap of paper in her clammy hand, she shakily compiled the second plate before delivering it to Luke.

"Perfect," he said, checking it, tidying it a smidge, then placing it on the pass, before slamming his hand onto the bell. "Service, table three, please!" Then, to her, "Well done. Thanks for jumping in there. Much appreciated."

"N-no problem." She gave a tight smile, then hurried back to her station, her heart pounding. Huffing out a breath, she swept her forearm across her sweaty brow. If that was how she reacted to the merest brush of his fingers against her hand, how was she going to be when he was full-on breathing down her neck as she dished up the desserts?

She watched in increasing dismay as plate after plate was ferried into the dining area of the café, since every one that went was a step closer to her finding out.

Chapter Five

"One roulade with regular cream, one Christmas pudding with brandy cream, and two cheese and biscuits," Luke read from the slip of paper, then looked up at her, his eyebrows raised in query.

She nodded to confirm she'd heard and understood, making her hat bell jingle, then took a deep breath and launched in to her task—aware he hadn't reeled off nearly as many orders at once as he'd done for the previous two courses, and incredibly grateful for it.

Luke appeared at her elbow. "What can I do?"

Scrunching her toes up inside her shoes to try to diffuse some of the tension caused by his proximity, she replied, "Could you sort out the cheese and biscuits while I handle the other two, please? It's all there, it just needs plating up."

"'Course."

They worked swiftly and silently, and ended up being neck and neck as they took their plates to the pass. As they drew closer and the space narrowed, Luke paused and indicated she should go ahead of him. She inclined her head graciously, placed the desserts on the pass, then hurried back to her station, ready for Luke to start calling out the next four. She grabbed a cloth and wiped up a couple of drips of cream from the worksurface, then glanced over just in time to see and hear Luke summoning the wait staff for that table, then striding back towards her, two paper slips in his hand.

"Excellent work," he said with a smile. "The desserts are looking great. I'd love to be able to say there's a slice of roulade with my name on it, but I very much doubt there'll be any left by the time we get to eat anything. Shame," he pouted playfully, then gave a slight toss of his head, making the bobble of his Santa hat bounce and sway, "you know I've always been a big fan of your roulade."

Unwilling to be drawn into that particular conversation, for fear of what else it might dredge up, Rosie instead smiled blandly at Luke and said, "What's next?"

He frowned and narrowed his eyes, clearly not expecting her cool response. Then, quickly recovering, he checked the topmost paper in his hand. "Another roulade and regular cream, two cheese and biscuits, and one who would like a couple of mince pies."

"Coming up." She started with the cheese and biscuits, which she then slid across the worktop in Luke's direction, hoping he'd take the hint and ferry them to the pass for her, since he was apparently so eager to help. Obviously, she was perfectly capable of taking them herself, but she really wanted to put some space between herself and Luke, even if just for a few seconds, *and* it meant she could crack straight on with the next two desserts. Everyone else had done so brilliantly, she didn't want to be the one to let them all down by serving too slowly, or putting out substandard dishes.

Thankfully, Luke wasn't too proud or up himself to protest, and he whisked the plates away before promptly returning for the next two. He also seemed to recognise her need to just get on with it, and didn't try to engage her in conversation again. He stayed in work mode, reeling off the orders, then delivering them to the pass once they were ready. A couple of adjustments had to be made when the roulade ran out, but fortunately nothing else did, and the affected diners got their second choice of dessert. They could hardly complain, though, since the roulade hadn't been on the menu to begin with. So, technically, they were still getting their first choice.

Finally, as the 'out' door flapped in the wake of the staff member carrying the final table's desserts, allowing in the undulating sounds of merriment and the easily recognisable Wizzard tune *I Wish It Could Be Christmas Every Day,* Rosie slumped exaggeratedly over her workstation with a grunt and leaned on her forearms.

"Phew!" she said, twisting her neck so she could peer at Luke, who stood a couple of feet away, his arms crossed over his chest and a shit-eating grin on his face. "I have no idea how you do that, day in, day out—and with way more complex menus and actual paying customers. I take my hat off to you. Truly." She pretended to doff the tiny elf hat on her headband.

Luke shrugged, but the slightest flicker on his face betrayed his pleasure at her compliment. "I'm used to it. It's certainly not for everyone—the frankly staggering amount of people who drop out of this line of work proves that—but if you really love doing it, it's much easier. Besides," he unfolded his arms and gestured around the kitchen, "I'm never doing it alone. I've always got a team around me—and none greater than this bunch." He pulled a face. "Better not tell my staff at the restaurant that, though. I'll have a revolt on my hands."

There was still plenty of hubbub with crockery, cutlery, glasses, trays and more being washed, dried and put away, so Luke clapped his hands and said loudly, "Well done, everyone. That went spectacularly well. A swift, top-quality service, with not an issue in sight, and very happy guests. I know it's already been said, but I honestly can't thank you enough for giving up your precious time, on today of all days. It's a wonderful thing you've done, and you should be very proud of yourselves. Of course, it wouldn't have been possible without In—oh, speak of the devil."

He stopped as Ingrid swept in, a bunch of empty plates and bowls in her hands. It looked as though dessert was going down just as well as the previous two courses. She deposited her load at the pot wash station, then turned to Luke with a pointed look. "What's this about me being the devil?"

Luke chuckled. "I was just saying as you came in that everyone's done a brilliant job, but that none of it would have been possible without you. You're the brains and the driving force behind this thing, so you deserve praise, too."

Brushing off Luke's words, but with her flushed cheeks giving her away, she jerked her thumb towards the doors leading to the main part of the café. "While I wholeheartedly agree everyone's done a brilliant job—more than brilliant, actually, but my brain's too fried to think of any more words right now—instead of taking our word for it, why don't you all come out and see your satisfied diners? Leave what you're doing for now, we can finish it afterwards. Come on." When no one moved, she repeated, "*Come on!*"

Rosie dropped to the back of the line as the kitchen staff headed out, both because she felt more comfortable there, slightly hidden away, *and* because it put her as far from Luke as possible. Now her brain was no longer preoccupied with preparing and serving up desserts, there was more room for unwanted thoughts. *Plenty* of room, as it happened. Unfortunately, they all seemed to rush in at once, leaving her incapable of sorting them into any semblance of order, much less dealing with them. It resulted in leaving her dazed, almost having an out of body experience, as Ingrid shepherded all the volunteers into one big group and encouraged the guests to show their appreciation.

The whoops, whistles, cheers and claps seemed muffled, like she was underwater, or wearing earplugs. She was vaguely aware of pasting a polite smile onto her face, and, dropping into autopilot, began clapping herself, as the other volunteers were, too.

Presently, Luke's voice cut through the noise. The applause died off. She followed suit, dropping her hands to her sides as he said, "Thank you, everyone. We're delighted you enjoyed your day. But," he angled his body towards Ingrid, "of course, none of this would have been possible if not for our fearless leader, organiser, whip cracker…" he paused to allow a ripple of polite laughter, "so please put your hands together one more time… for Ingrid!"

The cheering and applause went up again, growing increasingly raucous, and this time Rosie was fully present. She caught sight of John amongst the diners—easy enough, since he still wore the yellow paper hat. He was gazing at his son with shining eyes full of pride, an enormous smile on his face as he applauded. She tried to see if he had a wedding ring on, but she was on the wrong side of him and couldn't tell.

Rosie shoved the thought aside and smiled to herself at the touching display of fatherly love, then turned to peer through the group of volunteers towards Ingrid, smiling and clapping enthusiastically. The woman in question was clearly embarrassed at the attention, and stood awkwardly, her fingers laced together in front of her chest, and a bashful smile on her face.

Eventually, she was forced to hold her hands up and say, "Okay, okay, that's quite enough, thank you. Much more and you'll make me blush. Those of you who haven't already, please do finish your desserts. We'll start clearing away your empties and take orders for coffees, mince pies and jam tarts. If, of course, you're already full up, we've got tin foil galore so we can send you home with a doggy bag for your supper."

Ingrid gracefully extricated herself and scurried behind the counter, where she started prepping for coffees.

The wait staff returned to their tasks, and Luke made his way towards the kitchen, the rest of the kitchen team automatically following, so Rosie did the same.

"Right," he said, once they were all back together, "Hattie, Mac, Rosie—if you want to go and grab your stuff and get off, Chris and I can carry on with the clear up. I'm sure some of the wait staff will muck in, too, if they're hanging around for a feed."

While Hattie and Mac nodded and began removing their aprons, Rosie frowned and shook her head. "Er, no. I'm not leaving. I'm here for dinner, too, if there's enough left. I'm more than happy to help with the clearing up."

"Oh." Luke's brow creased. "Okay, if you're sure. I thought you'd be going to your mum and dad's."

He clearly hadn't been made aware of the series of events

which had brought her here today in the first place. Ingrid had probably had way too much going on to worry about letting him know. And why would she, anyway, since she hadn't realised Rosie and Luke knew each other at that point?

She shook her head again. "'Fraid not. Our Christmas was cancelled as they came down with a horrible bug the day before Christmas Eve. And James and his family live in Australia now, so we don't see them as often as we'd like."

Luke's expression dropped into one of sympathy. "Ah. Now the additional food you brought makes sense. Aww, that sucks. While I'm sorry your Christmas plans went awry, and I hope your mum and dad are all right, I'm really glad you're here. Not quite sure how we'd have managed without you."

"Ah, you'd have been fine," she shot back with a wave of her hand. "Anyway, what do you need me to do next?"

Taking the hint the conversation was over, Luke screwed his face up thoughtfully, then said, "Actually, do you want to discreetly find out how many are staying for dinner, please, so we can make sure we've got enough clean crockery, cutlery and whatnot? That way, we can start dishing up as soon as the last punters have gone. I don't want to leave it any longer than necessary, otherwise we'll be eating dried up meat and potatoes and gloopy gravy." He gave an exaggerated shudder. "Oh, and could you take the rest of the mince pies and jam tarts with you?"

"Yes, of course," she replied. "I'll get onto it."

She collected the relevant Tupperwares and whizzed out into the main body of the café, secretly glad to see things were winding down. Only a couple of people still picked at their desserts, while others were clearly waiting for their coffee and the goodies she was carrying. Hopefully that meant it wouldn't be too much longer before she could sit down to eat something, too. Her stomach was gnawing unhappily, and not just because of the Luke situation. If she could grab herself a nice meal, help clear up and get home for 6 p.m. and into her pyjamas, she'd be a happy bunny. There was a completely untouched tub of Cadbury's Heroes waiting on her coffee table—just one of the multiple types of confectionary she currently had in her house, a mixture of gifts and those she'd purchased herself. On top of that was the DVD of her favourite Christmas film, *Elf.* Next to those was a cinnamon spice candle. She could hardly wait to make use of all three in order to create the most perfect Christmas Night possible in the circumstances.

She placed the containers on the counter and turned to Ingrid, who was busily making coffees. "Mince pies and jam tarts here, Ingrid, whether people want them now or to take away. Also, Luke's asked me to find out how many volunteers are staying for dinner. I don't suppose you know, do you?"

Ingrid placed a coffee-filled glass onto a saucer, then wiped her hands down her apron and faced her with a smile. "I do, actually. Including myself, you and Luke, there will be six of us."

"Oh, good. That's saved me a job going around and finding out. Thanks."

"No problem. Could you take those in with you to be washed, please?" She pointed with her chin towards a crate of dirty dishes.

"Certainly can." With a smile, Rosie hefted the crate and made her way to the kitchen, pleased to learn there were a few others hanging around to eat. It might have been awkward with a smaller number, but six should be enough to keep the conversation flowing pretty effortlessly.

And it meant it was unlikely she'd have to be alone with Luke at any point, either. She was getting really tired now, and a chat with her ex, which would no doubt be at the least uncomfortable, at the most horrific, wasn't exactly at the top of her wish list. Small talk with the whole gang would be fine, but a serious conversation with Luke, not so much.

Chapter Six

Rosie sank into a chair with a deep groan of relief, both for her weary body and almost painfully empty stomach. A tall glass of strong coffee sat at her elbow—not her usual choice of beverage to go with a Christmas dinner, but she was in serious need of the caffeine, and didn't want to drink booze anyway, since she had to drive home. A luscious-looking prawn cocktail was in front of her, appearing more tempting by the second, but they were politely waiting on Ingrid to take her seat as Michael Bublé crooned quietly in the background and fairy lights twinkled all around them.

Ingrid, seemingly still full of beans—Rosie surmised she was running on adrenaline and would crash before long—whizzed out from behind the counter with a large coffee in one hand, which perhaps further explained her energy levels, and a box of Christmas crackers in the other.

They'd pushed two of the little tables together to make one larger one for the six of them, and she sat down at one end with a smug grin, placed her coffee down, then settled the box on her lap. "I made sure I bought enough for us, too. We've worked bloody hard today, I think we deserve some fun as well, don't we?"

"Absolutely," Luke replied from the opposite end of the table. Rosie had purposely dawdled when it came to getting her starter, hoping everyone else would take their seats before she did and mentally keeping her fingers crossed the last remaining place wasn't next to Luke. But, she'd figured, at least if it *was*, she'd sit there because she had to, not because she'd deliberately chosen to.

On this occasion, at least, the universe had smiled upon her and she'd ended up with Chris on one side, Ingrid on the other. "Thanks again, everyone. You really have outdone yourselves today," he added.

"Hey," Ingrid said, wagging a finger at Luke, "no more of that soppiness, now. We've said our thank yous, expressed our undying gratitude. Let's pull some crackers and eat something, shall we?" With that, she opened the box and handed the festive accessories around the table until everyone had one, then placed the box on the floor. "There. Everybody ready?"

The six of them assumed cracker-pulling positions with their neighbours.

Ingrid started the count. "One... two... *three!*"

Bangs and whoops filled the air, and Rosie giggled as she retrieved her prizes from the floor, where they'd tumbled when her cracker tore open.

"Hats on, folks," Ingrid commanded, while perching what Rosie thought was a rather fitting gold paper hat on her head. The queen of the café should wear a crown.

Doing as she was told, since defying her friend wasn't generally advisable, Rosie removed her elf hat headband and replaced it with her fuchsia paper hat before turning her attention to what turned out to be a tiny plastic yo-yo, an impossibly small deck of playing cards, then her all-important Christmas cracker joke.

"Oh, oh, I'll go first," Ingrid said, then chuckled as she peered at the tiny scrap of paper. "This is a good one."

Luke, now wearing a deep-green paper hat instead of his

Santa one, tutted. "Two minutes ago you were telling me not to be soppy so we could crack on with the food. Now you're insisting on reading out the bloody cracker jokes. Let's make this quick, Ingrid. My stomach thinks my throat's been cut, and poor Rosie looks fit to drop."

Rosie shot him a narrow-eyed look, not wanting to respond and potentially cause a scene or draw attention, but at the same time needing him to know she didn't appreciate his words. *Everyone* had worked their arses off all day without stopping to eat—why did he feel the need to point out she looked any worse than anyone else?

"All right," Ingrid said with a roll of her eyes. "Good to know we've got The Grinch at the table with us." She stuck her tongue out at Luke, then launched into her joke.

Within a few minutes, all the jokes had been read out and either laughed or groaned at, and Rosie was reaching for her cutlery when Ingrid gasped.

"Oh, I almost forgot!"

Luke threw his hands up, exasperation etched into his handsome features. "Bloody hell, Ingrid, we're going to be eating dessert at midnight at this rate. What now?"

While Rosie certainly wasn't going to voice *her* displeasure at the delay, she secretly agreed with Luke's disgruntlement. A glance around at the others indicated they felt the same.

"I just want everyone to raise a glass, that's all. It'll take a few seconds. *Grinch.*" She gave him a mock dirty look, then lifted her coffee. "Cheers to all of you. Merry Christmas!"

Everyone else hurriedly lifted their respective drinks, there were clinks and calls of "Cheers, Merry Christmas" all around, and sips were taken. Then silence reigned as they finally, *finally,* tucked in to their hard-earned meal. Rosie was surprised by the lack of chatter, but then maybe the others were as tired and hungry as she was, and therefore way more interested in eating than talking. Even Ingrid had piped down and begun devouring her pâté.

Rosie was so famished she had to consciously stop herself from wolfing her prawn cocktail down like a stray dog petrified someone was going to take their food away from them. Instead, she made sure to take her time and relish every bite. Thankfully, it had been worth the wait, and she hummed with pleasure as she set her cutlery down and reached for her coffee, before taking another sip. She cradled the glass, enjoying the soothing heat seeping into her fingers and palms and slowly drank the energy-giving liquid as she waited for the others to finish their first course. It didn't take long, and soon they were traipsing into the kitchen with their used plates and cutlery, adding them to the to-wash pile and grabbing clean plates to fill with their main course.

This was the part Rosie had been looking forward to most. She'd always been a sucker for a roast dinner, and, since a Christmas dinner usually had extra special treats like pigs in blankets and potatoes roasted in duck or goose fat, she was in heaven.

The group queued up and went along the hot plates like it was a buffet—a few quips being exchanged along the way—then reconvened at their table and dug straight in. Grunts and moans of gastronomical delight accompanied Chris Rea's *Driving Home For Christmas*, and as Rosie savoured a bite of a particularly crispy, delicious roast potato, she began daydreaming about doing just that. Much as she was enjoying the food, her social battery was beginning to run out and she found she couldn't wait to snuggle beneath a fluffy blanket on her sofa with a glass of wine, stick on the *Elf* DVD and crack open that tub of chocolates.

A change of song had her freezing with a forkful of turkey and stuffing halfway to her mouth. As the unmistakable opening bars of Mariah Carey's *All I Want For Christmas Is You* filtered out of the speakers, Rosie's mouth dried and her heart pounded. It was a good thing she hadn't taken the mouthful of food from her fork, because it would likely have stuck in her throat. Memories crashed into the forefront of her mind with the force and commitment of Wile E. Coyote smashing into a boulder he'd been tricked into thinking was the entrance to a tunnel.

It had been their first Christmas together, only a few months into their relationship, and they were still firmly in the throes of not-being-able-to-keep-their-hands-off-each-other passion. Since she'd still been living with her parents at the time, they spent most of their time at his place. Luke had been scheduled to work on Christmas Eve and Christmas Day, so they'd decided to pull their own celebrations forward by two days, when he was off. She'd shown up at his house in the evening after she'd finished work, her overnight bag in one hand and a gift bag containing his presents in the other. Little did he know what other surprise she had in store.

As he headed into the kitchen to pour them a glass of wine and grab some nibbles as the meal he'd prepared cooked, Rosie had placed his presents under the small tree in the corner, which they'd decorated together—eventually, after getting 'distracted' several times. Then she'd scurried into the bedroom, ostensibly to drop off her bag. While there, she ditched her socks—having already removed her shoes in the hallway—and the top layer of her clothes, leaving only the sexy new underwear set she'd bought recently underneath. In the en suite, she checked her hair and makeup. Then, satisfied, she'd grabbed the iPod she'd brought with her and slipped back into the living room, guessing correctly Luke was still in the kitchen, having found something he felt needed checking on, perfectionist that he was. She connected the iPod to his docking system, switched it on, cued up the song, then waited impatiently for his return.

The moment the adjoining door creaked, signalling Luke's imminent arrival, she'd pressed play. *All I Want for Christmas* began warbling out, and Rosie launched into the routine she'd been practising all week, every spare minute she'd got.

Luke had stepped into the room, then paused briefly as he spotted and processed what was going on. Then he'd placed two glasses of wine and a bowl of mixed nuts on the coffee table and dropped onto the sofa, the reflection of the Christmas tree fairy lights glinting in his eyes as he'd watched silently, intently, his elbows resting on his knees, chin resting on his knuckles. Heat filled her as she danced, and not just from the exertion. It felt like he was burning holes in her with his gaze.

He'd allowed her to go through the entire routine, complete with cheesy pointing at him for all the "you"s in the chorus, without saying or doing a single thing. She'd had no idea what he was thinking, whether he thought it was insane, cute, sexy, repulsive or what, but was determined to see it through anyway.

She found out only when the last notes had faded away. The sofa released a squeak of protest as Luke sat back. Then, his gaze still fixed on her, still full of heat, he lifted his right hand and crooked his index finger, beckoning her.

Rosie was powerless to resist. Not that she'd wanted to.

Later, as Luke had cradled a trembling, post-orgasmic Rosie in his arms, he'd dropped a kiss to her damp forehead and whispered, "I love you."

She'd gasped, snapped her head around to look at him. While she'd been feeling that way about him for ages, she'd never plucked up the courage to say the words. But since he'd said it first...

She'd grinned, tears of happiness welling in her eyes. "I love you, too."

"Well," he'd returned her smile, "this *is* turning out to be a merry Christmas."

Now, over a decade later, those once-happy memories made her stomach clench uncomfortably around the food she'd been so enthusiastically consuming, and the blood drained from her face. She knew, even without checking, Luke was looking in her direction. The weight of his gaze was tangible. Her knife and fork clanged onto her plate as she leapt to her feet so quickly her chair tumbled over backwards and crashed to the floor. "S-sorry. E-excuse me. I-I need some air."

Rosie skirted around the table, ignoring the open-mouthed stares, and stumbled towards the exit. It was locked, but after a couple of fumbled attempts at twisting the latch, Rosie succeeded, then threw herself at the door and gasped as it flew open, spilling her out into the December evening. She hadn't had the chance for so much as a glimpse out of the window since arriving at the café, but it seemed the rain had long since dried up. There was now a distinct nip to the late afternoon air and it was growing dark.

She pushed the door shut behind her and barrelled away from the café, with no idea where she was going, knowing only that she needed to get away from *him*, from the memories that blasted song had brought back. Of course, it wasn't the first time she'd heard it since their split—she'd endured it endless times in the festive periods of the intervening years—but, while the first few times had been triggering, she'd forced herself to deal with it. Eventually, hearing it had caused nothing more than a sad, wry smile and a little pang in her heart.

But that had been before she'd spent several unexpected hours in Luke's company, with thoughts and feelings swirling through her like a maelstrom the entire time, despite her attempts to ignore them. As far as she was concerned, she'd been coping relatively well, but the belting out of *that* song at a moment when she wasn't distracted, and when he'd been sitting right there, had thrown open Pandora's box, and now she was scurrying through the streets of her hometown, so quiet and deserted it was eerie, wondering how the hell she was going to explain her actions to the others—not including Luke, obviously, who had clearly known what was going on. Because she'd *have* to go back—her coat, bag, phone, car keys, and house keys were in the café, so she had no means of escape, and no way of calling for help. Technically, she could walk home from here—although it'd be a good forty to fifty-minute traipse in the dark—but with no way of getting into the house, it was pointless.

The same went for her shop at the other end of the high street—with no keys, all she could do was hunch in the doorway, feeling sorry for herself and probably looking like she was about to burgle the place. Her mum and dad's was further away even than her house, and while she knew they wouldn't turn her away, even in their poorly state, she still didn't want to risk picking up their bug. She had way too much to do at work in the next few days.

Her breathing rate increased, sending billowing clouds out in front of her face with every exhalation. *Fuck! What the hell am I going to do? I can't wander around the town centre all night like a drunk. Though at least perhaps today, of all days, if anyone saw me they wouldn't bat an eyelid.*

She was approaching the ginormous Christmas tree in the centre of the wide paved area that served as part of the town's outdoor marketplace, adorned in all its finery, when Luke's voice came from behind her.

"Rosie, wait!"

Bollocks. She didn't stop, didn't turn, only moved faster. He was the last person she wanted to see right now.

His growl was louder than his shout, making it sound as though he was gaining on her. "For fuck's sake, Rosie, *wait.* I've got your coat. At least put that on, even if you won't talk to me. Please."

His begging tone gave her the slightest pause, and that was all he needed, with his much longer legs, to overtake, then step in front of her and spin around, stopping her dead in her tracks. They were level with the tree now, and its flashing multicoloured lights illuminated Luke's face, clearly showing his concern. His paper hat had gone, and a thick jacket covered his upper body.

He shoved her coat at her. "Just put the bloody thing on, will you?"

She snatched it from him with a scowl and shrugged into it, not allowing her face to show her relief at the warmth and comfort it provided, then tugged off her cracker hat and stuffed it into her pocket. "Ugh, do you have to be so bossy all the time?"

Luke stepped forward, reached down, and carefully did up her coat's zip, slow and deliberate. The scent of his aftershave swirled around her, only serving to emphasise the power of the memories the music had brought forth. By the time the final few teeth cinched together beneath her chin, she was staring up into his face, her heart pounding and cheeks flushed. It was almost possible to forget they'd ever broken up as the urge to kiss him grew stronger.

He shifted his gaze the tiny distance from the top of the zip to her face, then smirked. "If I remember rightly, you used to like it when I bossed you around."

Chapter Seven

With a grunt of frustration, Rosie pushed past Luke and stomped across the marketplace, still without the faintest idea of where she was going, but just wanting, no, *needing* to be away from him. How could he be so blasé, so damn *cocky*, when he knew perfectly well what had upset her? Or perhaps he genuinely didn't. Perhaps what had been so monumental for her at the time hadn't been important enough to take up real estate in his memory. He certainly hadn't thought she was important when he'd hopped onto that plane without a second thought for her all those years ago.

She scowled at herself, at her own over the top reactions. It was a two-year-long relationship a decade ago, for heaven's sake, so why was she getting so het up about it? Sure, she'd been gutted at first, but she'd been young, and had eventually moved on. There'd been other boyfriends, though admittedly no one who'd stayed around for all that long. She wasn't sure why, nor had she been that bothered. However much she might have wanted them to, none of them had fired her up in the same way Luke had. She'd got lukewarm at best.

Had it been that whole "first love" thing? Or had subsequent men simply not been right for her? While she did believe in love, she didn't believe there was only one person out there for everyone—it didn't make sense to her analytical mind. Luke had been perfect for her, until he wasn't. But that didn't mean there wasn't someone else out there who was equally as perfect for her—possibly even *more* perfect. She just had to meet him. Of course, statistics weren't necessarily on her side, given the size of the global population and well, the globe. Her next Mr Right could be in the same town, or he could be in New Zealand. She had no way of knowing.

"Shit," Luke said, his footsteps heavy behind her, "I'm sorry, Rosie. I shouldn't have said that. It was stupid. I was trying to lighten the mood, cheer you up. Come back inside and finish your dinner. You've barely touched it and you must still be hungry." He drew up beside her, and kept pace as she continued stomping along the paved area, avoiding puddles as she went.

"Don't you bloody well tell me what I *must*," she ground out through clenched teeth. "Thank you for bringing my coat, that was kind, but I'd like you to leave me alone now, please." She paused, then couldn't resist adding, "We both know you're good at that."

Luke made a strangled sound and halted briefly, making him disappear out of her peripheral vision, then immediately reappeared. "And what, precisely, is that supposed to mean?"

Anger flaring, she rounded on him, pointing her finger in his face and rolling her eyes. "Oh, come *on*. You're a lot of things, Luke Adams, but thick isn't one of them. You know exactly what I'm talking about."

His brow drew low. "You mean… when I went away? To New York?"

"Bingo. Got it in one."

"B-but," his frown deepened, "I didn't *want* to leave you. I wanted you to go with me. For us to stay together. More than anything. Surely you remember I practically begged you to come with me. You're the one who refused."

"Because you were asking me to give up everything to go with you. All the sacrifice was on my side, and all the benefit on yours."

He opened his mouth, then closed it again. Looked around, then gently took her hand.

She started to resist, to pull away, but Luke tightened his grip ever so slightly and led her to a nearby bench. He released her hand, mopped up the rain droplets on the seat with his sleeve, then indicated she should sit down. "Please. Let's talk about this properly."

When he'd mentioned talking earlier, this wasn't a topic she'd thought would be on the agenda. "Why?" She wrinkled her nose and stepped back. "What's the point? It was years ago. You went, I didn't. Discussing it now isn't going to change anything."

"Because," Luke shrugged and sat down heavily on the bench, causing it to let out a creak of protest, "despite the passage of time, you obviously still have something to say about it. And I'd very much like to hear it." He fixed her in his gaze, paused a moment, then patted the seat beside him. "Please, Rosie. Get whatever it is off your chest. You'll feel better. Then you can come back inside and finish your food. What have you got to lose?"

"Oh, nothing much. Only my sodding dignity," she muttered, but took a seat anyway, deliberately leaving a decent gap between them.

"Good girl."

His words, and the purring tone of his voice almost made her jump up and scarper for the safety of the café, so reminiscent was it of the way he'd often spoken to her when they were in the bedroom—or anywhere else they happened to be getting frisky. Instead, she clenched her thighs and buttocks and braced the soles of her feet against the ground. It didn't make sense to let this opportunity pass her by. She was being given a chance to go over what had happened, with the wisdom of several more years under her belt, and whatever the opposite of the heat of the moment was. The cold of the past, maybe? She pulled a face. That didn't even make sense.

"Tell me what you meant," he said, either not noticing or ignoring her internal monologue and resultant facial expressions. "About me asking you to give up everything to go with me. And about the sacrifice being on your side, the benefit on mine."

Rosie took a deep breath, staring across the marketplace at the enormous Christmas tree, standing there in all its sparkly prettiness, blissfully unaware of what was taking place a few metres away. The sky had grown darker still, making the Christmas tree lights stand out more. She tracked their flashing and dancing for several seconds, waited for her heart rate to decrease a little, then half-turned on the seat to face Luke. "Well… it was all about you, wasn't it? About *your* career. There was no consideration for mine. It was an irrelevance. Not so much as a blip on the perfect landscape of your vision for the future."

Luke had been shaking his head as she spoke, and now took the chance to jump into the conversational gap she'd left. "That's not true, Rosie. I know how hard you worked at your degree, how you busted a gut to get into journalism. I was proud of you. Wanted you to go far and love your work as much as I did."

"Really? Because I remember you saying the job in New York was going to pay you so much I wouldn't *need* to work." She let out an unladylike snort. "As if I'd have coped with sitting around all day in a swanky penthouse apartment with nothing to do. I'd have been bored shitless."

Luke narrowed his eyes thoughtfully for a second, then his expression cleared as he seemed to come to some sort of realisation. "You're right, I *did* say that, but it's not exactly what I meant. I certainly wasn't expecting you to sit around all day with nothing to do. I knew that wouldn't be your cup of tea. I thought being there would benefit *both* of us. Thought you'd relish the adventure, the opportunity to explore, visit museums, galleries, bookshops, go for walks... at least until you got your work situation sorted. And then you'd have had all that cool stuff on your doorstep to write about."

"M... my work situation?" Rosie frowned. "What work situation?"

He shrugged. "I didn't know whether you would apply for a green card, some other kind of visa, figure out a freelance position, or what. Things never got that far, did they?"

"You weren't expecting me to be like a 1950s housewife, having your dinner on the table and a beer in your hand as soon as you walked through the door?"

Just then, the streetlamps pinged into life, the one situated behind their bench putting them in a spotlight. Not that it mattered—there was no one around to see them, performance or not.

Luke glanced briefly at the lamp, then shook his head and

recovered himself, before giving her a one-eyebrow-cocked, wide-eyed stare. "No, of course not. Why the hell would you think that? I know it was a long time ago, but as I recollect, outside of the bedroom we had a very equal relationship. Like I said, I wanted you to succeed in your career, love your career, as much as I did. If the roles had been reversed, if you'd been offered an opportunity to go and work somewhere amazing for stupid amounts of money, I'd have jumped at the chance to go with you. To support you. To have a crazy adventure."

"Y-you would?"

"Of course."

"Even if it meant giving up a job you loved?"

There wasn't even a millisecond's hesitation before he responded, "Yes."

"You'd have left your home, your family, your job behind… for me?" Saying the words out loud triggered a sense of awareness at the edges of her consciousness.

"Yes. Without a doubt. I don't know how good your memory is, Rosie, but I loved you, with every fibre of my being. Worshipped the ground you walked on. I was devastated when you said you didn't want to come to New York with me."

"But you went anyway. You can't have loved me that much."

Luke stiffened and fixed her with an exasperated stare. "Are you taking the piss? You *told* me to go. Said it was an amazing opportunity and I'd be crazy not to take it, but made a point of reiterating you wouldn't be joining me. From that, I very much got the impression you were done with us, especially since you walked out at that point and refused to see me, or answer my calls or messages. What was I supposed to do? Stay here on the off chance you didn't mean it? Run the risk of getting arrested for harassing you? Upset your parents by banging on their door at all hours? Also, saying I can't have loved you that much because I went could also be reversed. Maybe you didn't come with me because you didn't love *me* that much. Maybe it was precisely the excuse you needed to end things."

"I…" She cringed, then dropped her head into her hands and rested her elbows on her knees. "*Shit.* That wasn't the case at all, Luke. I never wanted to end things. I loved you with every fibre of *my* being, too. I think…" she blew out a breath, "I was just scared about leaving my life behind, everything that was familiar. I was young, and… I dunno, maybe a little immature? I didn't have the confidence to leave the safety net of my home and family. And since I was so new to my career, I thought I'd be risking ruining it before it had truly begun. Ugh, what a mess."

Silence wrapped around them so completely, the sound of continuing merriment from the café was just about audible.

She sighed, staring down at the paving slabs beneath her feet, then murmured, "Was it worth it?"

"Was what worth it?"

"Going to New York."

He paused for a moment before responding, "Yes and no."

Rosie straightened, then turned to look at him, her heart rate picking up again. "What does *that* mean?"

He gave a one-shouldered shrug. "In some ways it was, in

others it wasn't."

"Care to elaborate?"

The pained expression on his face said he didn't, but after a couple of deep breaths, which sent clouds of condensation billowing away from him, he finally said, "Career wise, it was the best thing I've ever done. But personally, it was a disaster. Possibly the *worst* thing I've ever done."

She arched an eyebrow, encouraging him to go on.

He pulled a face. "Really? You want all the gory details?"

"Obviously. Nosey, remember?"

He chuckled. "Of course I remember. The inquisitive journalist in you. Glad to see that hasn't changed." He took a cycle of breath, then, "The job was amazing. Every positive adjective you can think of, throw it out there and you're somewhere in the ball park. I had all the staff I needed, *more* than I needed. All the equipment, ingredients, budget. Creative freedom. The place did great—the Wall Street bods who financed it basically brought the customers in with them. Their friends, colleagues, acquaintances, business contacts. We didn't need to advertise, to try that hard to get bums on seats. People just came, spent obscene amounts of money, left, and told their rich friends. Who then came along, spent obscene amounts of money, left, and told *their* rich friends, and… well, you get it."

His expression told her there was more.

"But?" she prompted.

"It was an amazing success. *I* was an amazing success—it felt like I had the Midas touch. Every new dish, every innovation an instant hit. It was insane. I could do no wrong. No matter how wacky the idea. But…" he gave her a wry look, as if acknowledging she'd been right, "it was a hollow victory. While my career and bank balance were on the up, everything else sucked. I worked stupid hours—even for the hospitality industry—and went home to an empty, soulless apartment. I had no friends, no social life. My family was on the other side of the Atlantic. And, worst of all, I'd lost you. Sure, I was in one of the most exciting cities on the planet, with cash to splash, but I couldn't be bothered. I didn't have the energy or the enthusiasm. I suppose I was depressed.

"So I just kept working, and working. To distract myself, stop me having time to think about how fucking miserable I was. I thought maybe the continuing rise of my career would drag me kicking and screaming out of the doldrums. After all, how could a person who was at the absolute top of their game, getting amazing reviews and bringing in unbelievable custom be depressed?" He let out a humourless chuckle. "Then," his expression sobered so rapidly it sent a chill racing down Rosie's spine, "one day, I got a call from my dad."

Chapter Eight

Luke scrubbed at his beard and dropped his gaze to the ground.

This time, Rosie didn't prompt him to carry on. He'd already said some things that had clearly been very difficult, but this was on another level. Putting her own feelings aside to offer him the comfort he obviously needed, she reached out and took his hand, then squeezed it. "It's okay. You don't have to tell me."

After a beat, he met her eyes, and the emotion she saw there made her heart skip a beat, and an unpleasant thud land in her stomach. *Oh God, please don't say my bad feeling about his mum was right.* "I-I know. You..." he scrunched up his nose, "don't know already? From the grapevine?" he asked hopefully, probably wishing he didn't have to explain.

She shook her head. "Sorry, no. But I thought maybe something was amiss when I found out your dad came today... alone."

"Amiss. Ha. That's one way of putting it."

"Sorry." She squeezed his hand again. "I was just trying to tread carefully. Be sensitive."

He squeezed back, then gave her a thin-lipped smile. "I know. *I'm* sorry. Just dealing with things the Luke way—sarcasm, flippancy and dark humour."

"I remember," she murmured.

For several seconds he stared into her eyes, his own swimming with a mixture of pain and grief, then he huffed out a huge sigh. "He'd phoned me about Mum. She'd been rushed into hospital." He blinked slowly, then looked down at their linked hands and continued, "Apparently, she'd been complaining of a few health issues for a while. Nothing too bad, just niggles, according to her. She put them down to her age and got on with life. Didn't bother seeing a doctor. Then, one night she woke up in excruciating pain. Could barely speak, absolutely wet through with sweat. Dad couldn't get much sense out of her. So he somehow managed to get her out of her pyjamas and into some clothes and shoes, then bundled her straight into the car and took her to A&E.

"By the time he got parked at the hospital, she was going nuts with the pain. He couldn't get her out of the car by himself. So he had to lock her in, rush up to A&E and beg for help. Thankfully a porter was just coming back into the reception area with an empty wheelchair, so he dashed off with Dad and between them they got Mum into the chair and up to the A&E department. Meanwhile, the other staff had heard what was going on, and a doctor was waiting. They didn't have them hang around in the waiting room—they rushed her straight out the back and started running tests." He blew out a heavy breath and ran a hand through his hair. His other one had become increasingly tense beneath hers. "E-eventually, after ruling out diagnosis after diagnosis, they found the problem." With what appeared to be a gargantuan amount of effort, he lifted his gaze to hers. His eyes glistened with moisture. "C-cancer. She was riddled with it."

Rosie had had a horrible feeling that was where Luke's story was going as he'd been speaking, but hearing the words said out loud felt like a slap in the face regardless. A punch, even. Worse still, everything Luke had said so far, coupled with his body language, didn't imply there was a happy ending to the story. She clapped her free hand over her mouth as tears sprung to her eyes. "Oh, Luke…" She swallowed hard around the lump in her throat and whispered, "Your poor mum… Cathy. I'm so sorry. I… don't know what else to say."

"There's nothing else you *can* say. Nothing anyone can say. It was awful. Naturally, I got on the first flight to Heathrow, then jumped on the Tube, took a train and a taxi. On my previous visits home, Mum and Dad had always met me at the airport. The fact Dad didn't offer to come and collect me that time told me everything I needed to know. He hadn't given me the prognosis over the phone, and I hadn't asked. I guess I didn't really want to know, not yet. I already had enough to process. But when he suggested I might want to book the soonest flight I could get, I knew it was bad." He sniffed, and a tear escaped his right eye, ran down his cheek and disappeared into his beard. "By the time I got to the hospital, Mum was barely with it. She was clinging on to life, technically, but she couldn't speak, and only occasionally responded to stimuli. The doctors had her on some serious pain relief to make her comfortable.

"I-I arrived at just after three in the morning. Stinking, knackered and with no idea what the fuck was going on." The tears fell freely now, as did Rosie's. "But I g-gave her a kiss hello, then sat in the chair by her bed and held her hand, chatted to her. Utter bollocks, about nothing in particular, just on the off chance she might vaguely be aware I was there and take some comfort from it.

Dad held her other hand, looking utterly defeated. Haunted, even. About half four that morning, her breathing changed. We let the nurses know, and they said it was almost time and that we should say our goodbyes."

His next words were harder to understand as they came out so strangled. "W-we kept holding her hands, told her we loved her and that she should go wherever she needed to go, so she was out of pain. We p-promised we'd be okay, and would look after each other." He breathed in shakily, then let it out. "She slipped away peacefully about five minutes later." He scrubbed the back of his hand roughly across his eyes and face, mopping up the tears. "She was only sixty-fucking-three."

Rosie pulled her hand from his, then slid closer to him on the bench and drew him into a hug. "I'm so, so sorry," she whispered into his ear, her tears tumbling onto the shoulder of his jacket, "that's absolutely horrific." She cast wildly around for something else to say, but quickly came to the conclusion there was nothing to really add to that. Nothing she could say would make the situation remotely better. So she just held him tightly, stroked his hair, let him cling to her and cry it out. Who knew when he'd last allowed his grief a voice? If he even *had*. He had form for burying his head in the sand, after all.

Eventually, he sighed and sagged against her, then drew back, his expression full of chagrin. He sniffed and wiped the heels of his hands across his eyes and cheeks. "Sorry, Rosie. I never intended all that to come flooding out. It was like a bloody tsunami. Couldn't stop it."

She shook her head. "Don't be silly. You obviously needed it. When... did it happen?" From the age he'd said Cathy had been when she passed, she suspected not that long.

He swallowed audibly. "F-February. I ditched Valentine's Day at the restaurant to fly home. My bosses were *not* impressed."

"But... they were extenuating circumstances. Surely they understood?"

Luke shook his head sadly. "Not really. They might have been brilliant at giving me what I wanted resource-wise, but it turned out they saw me as just another one of those resources. Of course, it didn't help they'd had the best part of ten years of me working like a dog without even a whisper of complaint. Maybe they'd started to see me as a machine, rather than a man. With feelings, loved ones. Anyway, their unsympathetic reaction to my family emergency was the straw that finally broke the camel's back. Once I came home, I never went back."

"Seriously?" Rosie gaped at him. "You jacked it in, just like that?"

"Yep. They made it clear they didn't give a shit about me, so I decided it wasn't worth giving a shit about them."

"But what about your career? Weren't you worried quitting like that would affect your future prospects? And what about all the stuff in your apartment?"

He shrugged. "At that point, I was mired in shock, grief and depression, as well as suffering from burnout. I'd given my last flying fuck. I paid the building manager a handsome amount to clear my apartment and ship my belongings to me, rather than going back to do it myself. I was *done* with that place, and wasn't thinking about my future prospects. All I could focus on was the present, and making sure Dad was okay. Luckily, I was in a position to do so, since the restaurant had paid me so well. Beyond rent, bills and food, I'd barely spent anything. I knew I could move in with Dad, at least short term, and easily live off what was in my bank account until I sorted something else out."

"And you obviously did. Now you're here. I'm really, really sorry about your mum, but it is… nice to see you."

"Thanks. It's nice to see you, too," he said softly, giving her an almost shy smile. Then, his tone brighter, he asked, "So, let's change the subject to something more cheerful. What about you? How have you spent the last few years? How's the journalism gig?"

"Ah." She winced, then twisted her hands together in her lap. "About that…"

Luke's eyes widened. "Oh God, have I put my foot in it?"

"No, no, it's fine. The gig was good to start with. I enjoyed the research, the pitching, the chasing after jobs being a freelancer involved. And the writing, of course. But after a few years of that I began to want something more stable. You know, an actual regular, guaranteed salary, so I might actually be able to move out of my parents' place one day. But it soon became apparent to do that, *and* to write about stuff I was actually interested in, I would have to move away. Most likely to London. And… I wasn't up for it." She pulled a face. "Once again, I wasn't brave enough to make the leap. But honestly, that time I think it was the right decision. If my career had been fulfilling me *that* much, I'd have fought for it, wouldn't I?

"So, I carried on doing as much freelance work as I could, to keep some money coming in while I made other plans. Over the years, my work had taken me to all sorts of places, given me all sorts of experiences, in the name of research. Along the way, I fell in love with crafting and began doing it as a hobby. Knitting, sewing, crochet, felting. I soon started to wonder if I could somehow make my hobby into a job. Long story short, I could. I now own a shop at the other end of the high street. It's a collective hub—we sell all sorts of items from local makers. Mostly vintage and handmade, but really anything that fits the 'gift' or 'treating yourself' brief, and I'll consider stocking it."

Luke looked thoughtful for a moment, then his expression cleared. "Oh, wow. You mean The Creative Collective? That's yours?"

"You know it?" she replied, her eyebrows leaping towards her hairline.

"I do. I've never been in, but the window displays are always incredible. Very eye-catching. Your work?"

She nodded. "Mostly. I have a few part time staff who help me out in the shop, but I do the lion's share of the window displays, merchandising and whatnot."

"Nice that you're in a job which still allows you to flex those creative muscles of yours. Do you like it?"

"I love it. It hasn't always been easy, particularly during the pandemic, but being able to make and sell beautiful things, as well as providing a space for others to do the same, is amazing. Seeing people's faces when they come in and start poking around, finding all these wonderful treasures... well, it's probably how you feel when you see someone enjoying one of your meals."

"And is there time for... romance in what sounds like a very busy schedule?"

She snapped her gaze to his face. Why was he asking her *that*? Ignoring her skipping pulse, she replied, "N-no, sadly not. Well, I guess there's time, but not much inclination, to be honest. What about you? From what you've said, there wasn't anyone in New York, but how about now you're home?"

"I, er, don't know, actually..." He rubbed the back of his head and regarded her thoughtfully. "I didn't think so, but then I unexpectedly bumped into someone who used to be very special to me."

"Oh yeah?" Her pulse skipped faster. Was he talking about her? She didn't want to assume and risk making a total arsehole of herself. "And do you think... she could be special again?"

He took her hands and tucked them against his chest. Even through his layers of clothing she could feel his heart beating, faster than seemed normal. He stared into her eyes, intensity burning in their depths. Her stomach flip-flopped. If he *wasn't* talking about her, he was acting seriously fucking weird right now. "Honestly, she never *stopped* being special. She just wasn't around anymore."

"And now she is..?"

Luke squeezed her hands tighter, then leaned in, so close his warm, coffee-scented breath wafted over her face. "Now she is, well, let's wait and see what happens."

She closed her eyes at the familiar brush and tickle of his

beard on her face. Waited, excited anticipation racing through her veins, for his lips to contact hers. Clenched her thighs together when they did, her heart and core melting simultaneously. Goosebumps erupted over her skin, and she moaned.

Luke took advantage of her parted lips to deepen the kiss. As his tongue delved inside her mouth, he slipped his hands to the small of her back and drew her closer. She looped her arms around his neck in response, flinging open the door to her emotions as sensation rocked her body. Being in Luke's arms again felt like the beginning of an exciting adventure and coming home simultaneously. She had no idea how that was even possible, but it didn't really matter. All that mattered was the here and now, and the incredible kiss that was causing fireworks to go off inside her—mind *and* body.

Her skin was so flushed that when something cold landed on her face, she gasped into Luke's mouth and jerked away from him with a frown. "What—?"

They tilted their heads back and regarded the darkened sky, from which tiny white flakes were falling.

"Wow," she whispered, smiling. "It's a Christmas miracle."

"Yes," he gently gripped her chin and brought her head back down, before closing the gap between them once more, "it really is."

Chapter Nine

Rosie shivered, and not just as a result of Luke's mouth possessing hers.

He pulled back and looked at her questioningly. "Are you all right? Do you want me to stop?"

"No, it's not you. That was amazing. It's just… it's getting cold out here." The snow continued to fall. Already, Luke's dark hair and his jacket were dusted with flakes. She probably looked much the same.

He nodded, then disentangled from their embrace, stood, and held out his hand, his shoulders hunched up towards his ears. "Come on, let's get back inside and grab a hot drink. Maybe finish our meals."

She allowed him to pull her to her feet, then fell into step beside him as he headed for the café, still holding his hand, which was warm and strong in hers. "They'll be cold by now."

"You ever heard of a microwave?"

Rosie gasped. "Isn't that blasphemy, for a top-notch chef such as yourself?"

"Yes, if I was cooking something for a paying customer. I wouldn't dream of it. But for the purposes of reheating something for myself, and, in this case, you, I'll make an exception. It's not ideal, but it's better than being hungry. And we don't want the food to go to waste."

"True." It was part of the reason she'd volunteered today in the first place—so her excess food had a use, as well as creating work for her idle hands. "So," she added, as they drew closer to the Christmas tree, now adorned with a sprinkling of snow as well as lights and decorations, "how *did* you manage to get Christmas Day off from your restaurant? Isn't it usually all hands on deck in the hospitality business today?"

He glanced over at her with a wry smile. "I may... have played on my bosses' sympathies somewhat."

She arched an eyebrow. "Meaning..?"

"I dropped a lot of hints about it being the first Christmas since we lost Mum, mentioned my dad would be alone..."

"Not a lie, then."

"No." He shook his head. "Ingrid had already asked me to run the kitchen today before I even got the job at the restaurant, and I'd agreed—especially since Dad had said he'd come along to the meal, so he *wouldn't* be alone for at least part of the day. I just wanted to get my feet under the table a bit more before I sprung it on my bosses that I wanted arguably the most important day of the year off work. Thankfully, they were considerably more sympathetic than my previous employers."

"So, they know you've been cooking here today?"

He screwed up his face. "I didn't say that..."

Rosie pressed her lips and shook her head. "Such a rebel." She paused. "How do you know Ingrid, then?"

"We went to school together. Same class. What about you?"

"The independent businesses in the town are pretty tight-knit. Sticking together, cross-promoting each other and whatnot. I first met her when I was still in journalism, just from being around the town, keeping my ear to the ground, sniffing out potential news, but I got to know her more after joining in with some of the craft workshops she hosted at the café. She was actually the one who told me about the unit that now houses The Creative Collective becoming available. Now we're pretty good friends."

"Wow. Small world, eh?"

They reached the café, and Luke held the door open for Rosie, who flashed him a grateful smile before stepping with relief into the warmth. Everyone else had finished eating, and Luke and Rosie's plates had been cleared away. The wait staff who had stayed for the meal were cleaning tables and stacking chairs, while clanking from the kitchen told a story of washing up and putting away being done. The music had been turned off, making the atmosphere decidedly less cheerful than it had been earlier.

Ingrid emerged from the kitchen, a crate of clean glasses and mugs in her arms. She paused briefly on spotting them, then smiled. "Oh, there you are." She flicked her gaze between them. "Everything all right? I was about to send out a search party."

"Everything's fine," Luke said evenly.

"Sorry for running out—and for not mucking in with the clear up," Rosie added.

"Oh, don't worry about that," Ingrid replied, continuing on her way to the counter, placing the crate down, then slipping behind the counter to start putting the glasses and mugs away. "I'm just glad you're both okay. We covered your plates and put them in the kitchen."

"Thanks. Tell you what," Luke glanced around, then turned

back to Ingrid, "to make up for our disappearance, why don't you guys head off? Rosie and I are going to microwave what's left of our dinners, have some dessert, then we'll finish up the jobs that are left and lock up. Is that all right with you, Rosie?"

Pinned by his gaze and clamouring to catch up with his sudden and unexpected suggestion—the bit about locking up, at least—she blinked. "Er, yes, of course." Not so long ago, she'd been desperate to get away from him and indulge in a cosy night on the sofa with a tub of chocolates and her favourite film, but now she'd done an about-turn. While their kiss had been incredible, it had raised a whole bunch of questions, and she really wanted some answers. That'd be a damn sight easier if they were alone.

Ingrid looked up with a frown. "Er, are you sure? I mean, I don't think there's that much left to do, but—"

"We'll take care of it," Luke put in smoothly, then gave her a stare laden with meaning.

Ingrid peered between the two of them again. After a second or two, realisation dawned on her face. She smiled. "Ah, all right. I see. You'll turn everything off, lock up properly and set the alarm?"

"We will," he assured her. "We've both got experience of shutting up and securing properties for the night, remember?"

"Of course you have. Sorry. Control freak, remember? Okay, let me just empty this crate and I'll start rounding up the troops."

Luke nodded, then dashed off to stop one of the waitresses before she upended the chairs at the last remaining table. "Could you leave that one, please? Rosie and I are going to sit there and finish our meals."

"Okay," she replied with a shrug. "I'll leave the cleaning spray and cloth on the counter, then."

"Thanks."

"Well," Rosie said to no one in particular, "guess I'll take my coat off again, then." She joined Luke at the table, shrugged out of her coat, and hung it on the back of a chair. "Shall I make some hot drinks while you microwave the food?"

"Sure. Good idea." He removed his jacket and hung it on the back of the chair next to hers.

"What would you like?"

"A hazelnut latte would go down a treat."

"Coming right up."

They went their separate ways, and Rosie stepped behind the counter and squared up to the behemoth of a coffee machine, instantly regretting her offer to make hot drinks. "Er, Ingrid? Any chance you could show me how to use this thing? It's got more buttons than my TV remote. And I don't know what most of *those* even do."

Ingrid materialised at her side, grinning widely. "Only if you tell me what's going on with you and Luke. When you said you knew each other years back, I take it you meant *knew each other*?" She wiggled her eyebrows saucily.

"Well, yes," she whispered, glancing worriedly towards the kitchen door, "we were a couple, actually. For two years. But it… didn't work out."

Ingrid raised her eyebrows, then her expression turned decidedly unimpressed. "*Didn't work out?* Is that why you took off halfway through your meal? I'm going to need more information, honey, but another time, okay? You come and see me for a coffee and a chat later in the week, all right?" She rubbed Rosie's arm and gave her a warm smile.

"I will."

"Hmph. You'd better." She eyed Rosie sternly. "Right then, what do you want to make?"

A few minutes and with a load of what Rosie had always felt was unnecessary racket from the coffee machine later, she thanked Ingrid and headed for their table, a latte in each hand, while Ingrid made for the kitchen with her empty crate. Someone had laid the table, and she put their drinks down in their places, before taking a seat.

Luke arrived moments later with two plates, steam rising from them. After placing them down in the relevant spots, he sat beside her and picked up his knife and fork. "Tuck in—before it gets cold. *Again.*" He gave her an amused look.

She tutted and rolled her eyes, then scooped up her cutlery and inspected the plate of food she'd barely started. It didn't seem much worse for wear following its abandonment and a blitz in the microwave, and she *was* still hungry. The turmoil of earlier over and done with, for now at least, she started to eat. Thankfully, it was only a smidgen less delicious than it had been earlier. As she chewed and swallowed her third mouthful, the rest of the gang sloped out of the kitchen, smiling a little too widely and nodding at Rosie and Luke as they passed through the café on their way to collect their belongings from the staff area out back.

Waves and goodbyes followed as they disappeared out into the night, exclaiming as they spotted the snowfall on the ground, and the flakes still tumbling from the sky. From the brief glimpse Rosie caught through the open door, it was falling faster and more heavily still. A whoosh of cold air rushed in through the gap, before the last person tugged the door closed behind them.

She shivered, then frowned—snow hadn't been in the forecast, so she had no idea whether the council would have gritted the roads or not, or if the amount warranted ploughs being deployed. Even if they were, it would only be on the main roads. It would probably be wise for her and Luke not to hang around for too long, lest they run into trouble on their journeys home. They got so little snow in these parts, people weren't used to driving in it—including her, which made her nervous.

Ingrid approached their table, zipping up her coat. That done, she hooked her handbag over her shoulder. "Right, I'll be off then. Enjoy the rest of your dinner. And thank you again for today, I really appreciate it."

"Hey," Luke said, shooting a doubtful glance towards the door, and lowering his knife and fork to the table before starting to get up, "do you want me to walk you to your car? It's dark out."

Ingrid fluttered her hand at him, indicating he should stay in his seat. "Thank you, that's lovely, but not necessary. I will be absolutely fine." She smiled. "Okay, so you've got the alarm code, and you'll drop the keys to me on your way to your dad's? You won't forget, will you? I need them tomorrow as I'm taking advantage of being closed for a few days to pack away the Christmas decorations and have a deep clean. So while it'd be great if you could wash, dry, and put away the pots you use, clear and wipe down the table, and upend the chairs, don't worry about the floors. I'll do those when I'm cleaning."

"You'll have the keys back this evening," Luke replied, retrieving his cutlery. "I'll stick them through your letterbox."

"Great. I'll leave you to it, then. Toodles!" She waggled her fingers, treated them to a big beaming grin, pulled on a woolly bobble hat, then swept out.

The heavy thunk of the door seemed to underline that they were alone once more. They exchanged an awkward smile before returning to their food and eating in silence.

After a few bites, Rosie chuckled. "Well, I can honestly say this is the weirdest Christmas dinner I've ever had. And that's saying something—you've met my family!"

Luke echoed her chuckle. "I have. How are they all, anyway? And how did James end up moving to Australia? Does he like it there?"

They continued on light, superficial topics during their main course and dessert. Part of Rosie itched to ask the questions she so desperately wanted answers to, but a bigger part wanted to just enjoy the food and Luke's company. Top off Christmas Day on a happy note, rather than an uncomfortable one. So she kept her questions to herself.

Once they finished eating, they did as Ingrid asked, leaving everything clean and tidy, before going around making sure everything was switched off.

Finally, they shrugged into their coats, grabbed their belongings, and convened at the front door of the café, after Luke had retrieved the keys from wherever Ingrid had stashed them before she left. He held the door open, since Rosie's arms were full of the plastic containers she'd brought with her what was only hours ago, but felt like eons—though they were empty now, the food all consumed, right down to the very last two mince pies, which she and Luke had had with their desserts. With a murmur of thanks, she stepped into the night, gasping as the freezing air slapped her in the face.

She cringed and clamped her elbows into her sides. "Bloody hell, it's even colder than it was earlier. And look at that *snow*!"

A series of beeps came from inside the café as Luke set the alarm, then he scooted out next to her and pulled the door closed, before locking it. "Oh God, it is, isn't it? And when was the last time there was this much snow around here?"

She shook her head. "I can't remember. Years. And definitely not on Christmas Day. It's more likely to show up in January or February these days, sometimes into March."

"Maybe I brought it back from New York with me. It's a more frequent occurrence over there."

"Maybe."

They didn't speak for a few seconds, while they waited to hear the final tone from the alarm to indicate it was set correctly. Then Luke held out his arms for the containers she carried. "Give me those. I'll take them to your car."

"It's okay, I can manage. They're not heavy."

He tutted and rolled his eyes. "I know you can manage. I'm just making excuses to spend more time with you, all right?"

Rosie lowered her head as her cheeks flushed, and allowed him to take the containers. "Thank you. My car's in the car park at the end."

"Come on then," he said softly, "let's get you safely on your way home before this weather gets much worse."

They crunched their way carefully along the snow-covered pavements, past darkened shops, some with shutters pulled tightly closed, others with their uncovered windows looking like portals into a creepy abyss. Rosie averted her gaze, and focused firmly on the ground in front of her, on the lookout for any additional hazards that might be lurking under the snow—she didn't want to slip or trip, making a fool of herself, or worse, getting hurt.

There were streetlamps along their route as well as in the car park, and they reached her vehicle without incident. She reluctantly pulled her hands from her pockets so she could retrieve her car keys from her bag. If she hadn't been so distracted, she'd have thought to do that before leaving the café. Mentally shaking her head at her own stupidity, she pressed the central locking button, then made her way around to the boot and opened it.

Luke followed, placed the containers inside, then reached up and pulled the boot closed again. "There you are," he said with a smile as it *whumped* into place, "all sorted."

She returned his smile. "Thank you." Glancing up, she added, "I can't believe it's still coming down like this. But at least it started after all today's guests were safely home." She blinked to remove a couple of snowflakes that had landed on her eyelashes.

"Yeah." Luke grimaced. "The idea of some of that lot outside in this doesn't bear thinking about. Too many walking sticks and fragile bones for my liking."

They lapsed into a brief silence, before breaking it simultaneously.

"Well, I should—"

"Do you want to—?"

Luke indicated she should speak first.

"Oh," she peered down at her feet, "I, er, was just wondering if you wanted to come back to mine for a bit?" Looking up and meeting his eyes with a grin, she added, "I'm planning to watch *Elf* and crack open a box of Cadbury's Heroes." If he agreed, they could still keep things light, still end Christmas Day on a happy note. The tricky stuff they'd undoubtedly have to deal with could wait.

Luke groaned, a pained expression on his face. "Rosie, I wish I could, really I do, but… my dad. I know he's had company for a few hours today, as well as a decent meal, but I don't want to leave him at home by himself, tonight of all nights. He's coped admirably with losing Mum, to be fair, but you know what they were like at Christmas—it's probably hitting him quite hard."

"And you, too," she said softly, recalling the fun festivities she'd enjoyed in the Adams household in Christmases past.

He ran a hand through his hair, then dropped it to his side and shrugged. "Well, yeah, but I've been able to keep myself busy, haven't I?"

Rosie slipped her car keys into her pocket and took his hand.

"Yes, but it's perfectly okay to allow yourself to grieve, too, you know." She linked her fingers with his and squeezed gently. "I'm sorry, I shouldn't have asked you to come to mine. It was selfish of me. You *should* be with your dad tonight. Spend some time together, lean on each other. Talk about your mum. Share memories. Have a laugh. Or a cry. Whatever you need. Just let it out. It's cathartic."

With a lopsided smile, he squeezed back. "When did you get so wise?"

"Oh, I don't know about wise. I just know a little bit about grief."

He studied her for a moment, a line appearing between his eyebrows as he clearly tried to work out what she was alluding to. His frown deepened as something occurred to him. "But you'll be at home by yourself—on Christmas Night. Why don't you come to Dad's? He won't mind. You know he adores you. He always has. I'll bet he was gutted he didn't get chance to chat with you today."

Rosie lifted his hand and pressed a kiss to his knuckles, then let go and stuffed her increasingly chilly hands into her pockets. "Aww, that's sweet, Luke, but no. You and your dad need to spend this time together privately, not with me as a third wheel. Plus," she jerked her head towards the still-falling snow, "this is only going to get worse. I'm already a bit freaked out about driving in it, to be honest, so I think I should get home sooner rather than later. And so should you—especially since you've got to go via Ingrid's to drop off the keys."

"Yeah," he replied, his tone resigned, and put his own hands in his pockets. "You're right. About Dad *and* the weather. I just…

it's been great catching up. I don't want it to end, that's all."

She smiled. "Nor do I. But you're living back here now—we can see each other again whenever we like, can't we?"

"Yes, absolutely. I'd love that."

"Me too."

They grinned at each other through the swirling flakes, but didn't speak. Eventually, Luke cleared his throat, moved around the car and opened the driver's door. "Drive safely, won't you?"

Rosie followed him, then stretched up on her tiptoes and pressed a kiss to his cheek. "Thank you. Yes, I'll drive safely. You too. Merry Christmas." She got into the driver's seat.

"Merry Christmas." He checked her feet were inside the vehicle, pushed the door shut, then backed up a couple of paces and waited while she pulled out her keys, stuck them in the ignition and fired up the engine. The windscreen had a decent covering of snow, but luckily not so much the windscreen wipers couldn't handle it. She really didn't want to have to get out and scrape the snow off manually. She switched the wipers on, as well as the heater, then waved at Luke through the side window while she waited for the glass to clear.

Knowing he'd be a gentleman and wait until she drove away, and not wanting him to hang around any longer in the cold, she checked the windscreen, found she had just enough visibility to navigate the roads safely, then gave him a final wave before setting off into the night.

It wasn't until she pulled up on her drive some fifteen minutes later, following a taxing, scary journey which only took half that time when the roads were clear and not covered in snow, that she realised something.

She and Luke hadn't exchanged phone numbers. She'd deleted the one he'd had while they were together from her contacts a long time ago, to stop her from being tempted to get in touch with him and making an idiot of herself. And, if he still had her number from back then, it was irrelevant, since there'd been some sort of technical fault when she'd switched service providers a few years ago, and rather than keeping her number as she'd wanted to, she'd been forced to take on a new one. He famously hated social media, too, so unless he'd changed in that regard, she was pretty much stuffed. For now, anyway. There were ways and means of getting his contact details, but not ones she was willing to exploit on Christmas Night.

They'd been apart for a decade. A couple more days without being in touch wouldn't hurt.

Chapter Ten

Thanks to the weather, Rosie arrived at The Creative Collective a good couple of hours later than she'd intended to. The snow had eventually let up sometime overnight, but the view she'd been treated to when peering out of her window on Boxing Day morning was one of a glorious winter wonderland. No one on her street had ventured out yet, leaving the thick covering of snow completely pristine—marred by neither tyres nor foot or pawprints. It looked beautiful, but cold, so she decided to wait until the temperature increased, and hope the main roads had been well used by the time she reached them. The sun remained obstinately behind a sky packed full of grey clouds, so she didn't hold out much hope of any thawing going on.

After a hairy journey off her estate, followed by a slightly better journey on the main roads—which had been ploughed and gritted—she parked in the tiny staff-only car park behind The Creative Collective and heaved a sigh of relief. She got out of the car, locked it, and picked her way cautiously across the snow-covered tarmac, her hands, clutching both car and shop keys, stuffed deeply into her coat pockets. She wore warm winter boots with good grip, but since the car park was tucked in between buildings on three sides, it meant that, while it had been protected from some of the snowfall, no sunlight—should the sun deign to venture out in the first place—would land on the surface either, and hadn't done so all morning, meaning there was a chance it resembled an ice rink. Thankfully, the snow had remained fluffy, and each of her steps resulted in that lovely, satisfying crunching sound, making her grin to herself as she trod a path to the shop door, in spite of the bitter cold stinging the parts of her face not covered by her woolly hat and scarf.

She reached the building without incident, and let herself in—immensely grateful for the fact she could access the shop's heating system via an app on her phone, meaning she'd been able to turn it on before leaving home, so she had the benefit of arriving to a nicely-warming-up space, rather than a chilly one. She stamped the snow off her boots and wiped them on the mat, then locked the door behind her. It was unlikely there'd be anyone hanging around the town centre on Boxing Day, since almost everything was shut, but it always paid to be careful.

After deactivating the alarm, she flipped on all the shop floor lights, since there was so little natural light coming through the large front windows. Then she made her way to the till counter and stashed her handbag underneath it, before taking off her hat and scarf and placing them beside her bag. She decided to keep her coat on, just until the heating kicked in some more. She'd soon get warmed up when she started work.

Hands in her pockets, she surveyed the main body of the shop, making a mental plan of action. As well as taking down the Christmas decorations, she needed to re-do both window displays, then set about either pricing down the leftover Christmas stock, or putting it in the stock room. She also had a list of reductions across Christmas lines from her local makers—most of them preferred to try to clear what items were left, rather than coming to collect the stock and storing it themselves for another nine or ten months. She'd create an eye-catching display near the front of the store and hopefully draw in some bargain hunters.

Nodding to herself, she retrieved her phone from her pocket to put some music on, and remembered she'd promised to text her mum and let her know she'd arrived safely. They'd spoken on the phone the previous night, with Rosie eventually confessing what she'd actually done all day—leaving out the fact Luke had been the chef, and anything else to do with him. Her mum had been surprised, but proud, and had told Rosie she and Rosie's dad were on the mend, thanks to lots of rest and the delicious meals Rosie had left for them. They'd pencilled in their Christmas Day re-do for Sunday—three days away, providing they continued to feel better.

She pulled up a new message to her mum. *Just got to shop. Left home later than planned in hopes temperature would be higher to melt snow. Estate roads bad, main roads fine as been ploughed and gritted. Work car park okay. Hope you and Dad are still feeling better. Looking forward to seeing you Sunday. xxx*

After sending the message, she connected her phone via Bluetooth to the shop's speaker system, then went into her music app, pulled up her favourite, highly-curated playlist and hit the 'shuffle' button. A cheerful ABBA song piped out, and Rosie immediately whacked the volume up, since it was still set to the level they had for background noise while the shop was open to customers. The awesomeness that was ABBA always ought to be played loud, in her opinion.

Grinning, she put her phone on the counter, then took off her coat. Thanks to the spirit-lifting music, already the task ahead of her didn't seem so daunting. Swaying her hips exaggeratedly and singing along to the song, she made her way to the back room to retrieve the stepladder. After putting it up by the front door, she returned to collect the storage boxes for the decorations, which took a couple of trips. Finally, she was ready to crack on.

She worked methodically from the front of the shop to the back, taking down fake mistletoe, garlands and bunting, and stashing away cute festive signs, ornaments, and strings of colourful lights. Two storage boxes were already full to bursting, so she sealed them and put them away out the back. As she returned to the shop floor, ready to strip and pack down the Christmas tree tucked into a corner, she gasped as movement by the front door caught her eye. Her heart lurched painfully, and she blew out a breath and clutched her chest as she crept over to the door, wondering who the hell was hanging around in a deserted high street that lay under several inches of snow. A dog walker, maybe? Or a homeless person? She had some cash on her, but wasn't sure how much use that would be. Was there even anywhere open to buy food or a hot drink today? She didn't know. Though she had brought snacks for herself, as well as something for lunch, so could easily share those. And of course there was tea, coffee and hot chocolate in the staff room, as well as long-life milk, so a hot drink would definitely be on offer. It wasn't perfect, but it was better than nothing.

As she grew closer, and peered into the gloom, she made out the shape of a person, which became clearer as the distance between them decreased. Their lack of canine and their clean attire counted them out as either dog walker or homeless person, but the beam of the shop lights meant it wasn't until they pressed their face right up to the glass of the door that it dawned on Rosie who was out there.

"Luke! What the hell?" She gaped, held up her index finger to him to indicate she'd be right back, then hurried to the counter. She tapped her phone to wake the screen, pressed 'pause' on the music, then retrieved the shop keys from her coat pocket. With trembling hands, she unlocked and opened the door, then stepped back to usher him inside, her heart racing with shock and excitement at seeing him again—albeit much sooner than she'd expected. She quickly closed the door behind him, not wanting to let any heat out, then locked it again.

A pair of smiling eyes crinkled at the corners were about all that was visible from beneath a woolly hat and pulled-up snood. It was a wonder she'd recognised him at all. *No, it wasn't,* she chastised herself. *You know damn well you'd recognise those eyes anywhere.*

"Morning." He stamped his feet and wiped them on the doormat, then pulled his snood down to tuck beneath his chin and flashed her a grin. "Thought I'd find you here."

"Er, yes," she said, blinking in surprise, even as warmth at his proximity filled her being. "I'm here. But how did you know?"

"You mentioned something yesterday about getting the shop ready for reopening. I did try to call you, but I'm guessing you have a different number, as all I got was a recorded message saying the number I'd dialled was out of operation."

"Y-yes. I swapped providers a few years ago, and something

went screwy and they couldn't port my number across. It took ages to update my details everywhere and let people know. So annoying." She tried not to dwell on the fact he'd still had her number—albeit one that was out of service—a decade after they'd split up, particularly since she couldn't say the same. She forced a weak laugh. "It occurred to me last night we should have exchanged numbers, but I stupidly didn't think about it until I got home. I was going to text Ingrid and get your number from her." She mentally crossed her fingers he'd changed his number at some point, too, meaning he wouldn't immediately realise she'd deleted the old one.

His smile widened. "Well, I've saved you a job." He pulled his phone from his coat pocket and handed it to her. "Let's not make that mistake again, eh? Pop your new number in there for me, then ring it, would you?"

Her hands still way unsteadier than she'd have liked, she did as he asked. Seconds later, her phone trilled from across the room. "There," she ended the call, then passed his phone back to him with a tentative smile, "all sorted. Maybe it's just as well I didn't have to ask Ingrid for your number—she already made me agree to go and see her later in the week for coffee, so she can pump me for information about what happened yesterday and how you came into it. I don't want to give her anything else to interrogate me about."

Luke snickered. "Yeah, I suspected she'd be eager to find out all the gossip. Why do you think I said I'd put the café keys through her letterbox last night, rather than knocking on the door and handing them over in person?" He tapped his temple. "Not just a hat rack, you know."

She grinned. "Clever. Though I suppose I can't blame her. I'd be exactly the same if the roles were reversed."

"Obviously. Once a nosey sod, always a nosey sod."

With a wide-eyed gasp, she swiped playfully at his arm, but encountered little more than the thick down insulation of his puffer coat. "Cheeky git."

He shrugged. "Just saying it like I see it. You know me. Anyway," he gave her his sweetest, most hopeful smile, "any chance of a cuppa?"

She screwed up her lips and gazed doubtfully around her. On the one hand, she'd been plagued by thoughts of him ever since they'd parted ways the previous evening, wondering just what was going on between them, if anything. On the other hand, she still had a business to run, and all her tasks needed to be completed before the shop reopened in the morning. She'd prefer those tasks not to take her until that evening, or beyond. "I don't mean to sound rude, or like I don't want to see you, but... I've got quite a lot to do here." She couldn't bring herself to send him away, though. Not when he'd come out in the cold and the snow to speak to her. "Maybe just a quick one?"

"May I propose a counteroffer?"

She quirked an eyebrow, intrigued. "Go on..."

"We take our time with one cup of tea. Then I help you with whatever you need to do today. For..." he checked his watch, "a few hours, at least. I'm due in at work this evening. How does that sound?"

Rosie huffed out a breath and let her shoulders sag with

relief. She smiled. "It sounds great. Perfect, actually. I started later than I wanted to because of the weather, so any help to get back on track is much appreciated." She reached past him and locked the shop door, then pulled the keys out before returning them safely to her coat pocket. "Come on, let's go to the staff room and I'll get the kettle on." She made her way through the shop, with Luke following. A glance over her shoulder revealed him to be checking the place out as he walked, and she remembered him saying he'd not been in before.

"Do you always do this by yourself? Sort out all the post-Christmas stuff, I mean?"

She nodded as she passed through a door at the back of the shop and switched on the light. The small but well-appointed staff room blinked into visibility. "It's a tight turnaround to get it done before reopening on the twenty-seventh, but I can't bring myself to ask anyone else to come in to work on Boxing Day. Everyone's either still having family time, or quiet time in order to recover from the family time. Speaking of which," she indicated he should take a seat at the table, while she headed for the drink-making facilities, "how did yesterday evening go with your dad? Was he all right? Were you?" She filled the kettle, then switched it on before pulling out a clean mug to go with the one she'd already used several times since arriving at the shop that morning.

"You know what," he replied, as he took off his coat and hung it on the back of the chair, then sat, "it was... good." He removed his hat and snood, and placed them neatly on the table. "We talked about Mum, but in a positive way. Fun times, Christmases past, holidays, parties—that kind of thing." He paused. "He asked about you, too."

Chapter Eleven

Rosie finished putting sugar in the second mug, left the teaspoon in it, and slowly turned to lean her back against the worksurface as she waited for the kettle to boil. She adopted a casual tone as she replied, "Did he? What did he say?"

Luke gave her an amused glance, apparently seeing right through her feigned coolness. "He asked why I hadn't told him you'd be there. He was quite annoyed about it. I had to explain I didn't *know* you were going to be there, that I was just as shocked as him to see you. He then went straight for the jugular and asked if you were single and if we were getting back together. And added that you hadn't changed a bit."

She snorted. "Yeah, right. I'm older," she laid her fingertips at the edges of her eyes and pulled them down to iron out her laughter lines, then patted her stomach, "and fatter."

"Pfft," came the response. "What nonsense. I've never heard such utter bollocks in my life. You look as gorgeous as you always have. More gorgeous, actually."

Heat rushed into her cheeks, and she peered at him shyly through her lashes. "Thanks. You look pretty damn good yourself." *Understatement of the century.* She paused, then swallowed hard and forced out a version of the question that had been on her mind since the previous evening. "And what did you say when he asked if we were getting back together?"

He didn't reply straight away. Instead, he got to his feet, crossed the room and stood directly in front of her, forcing her to tilt her head back to look up at him. Her tummy fizzed at the seriousness in his eyes. "I was honest with him. I said it was the first time I'd seen you in a decade, that after we'd got over the shock of seeing each other, we'd done a little talking, but we probably had lots more ground to cover before getting back together was even a possibility." He gently took her hands and held them in his, making her stomach do a loop-de-loop. "But I also said if it *did* happen, I'd be the luckiest man on the planet."

The kettle reached its crescendo, then clicked off, drawing Rosie's attention.

Luke caught her chin and turned her head back to face him. "Rosie?"

"Y-yes?" she croaked, her mouth suddenly dry. How was it even possible that approximately twenty-six hours ago, she hadn't thought about Luke in a while, certainly not at any length, and hadn't even known he was in the country. And now he was here, right in front of her, and them getting back together was on the table. No wonder her head was spinning.

"What do you think?" he murmured, still cradling her chin. He brushed the pad of his thumb over her lips, making her tummy fizz more furiously, then released her chin and took her hand again. "Did I say the right thing to Dad? *Is* there a possibility of us getting back together, however distant it may be in the future?"

She swallowed again, trying to coax some moisture into her mouth. "I-is that what you want?"

Luke cocked his head and stared at her incredulously. "Are you seriously asking me that?" He lifted their joined hands and clasped them to his sternum, and pinned her in his intense gaze, making her want to squirm. "Rosie, I never wanted to split up in the first place. If things between us back then had gone how I wanted them to, we'd be married by now. Hopefully with kids." He blinked and shook his head. "I don't think you ever quite realised how strongly I felt for you. *Still* feel. Christ, Rosie, there's been no one since you. Not emotionally, anyway. Don't get me wrong, I haven't been a monk. I've had a handful of flings, some one-night stands, but no one ever came anywhere close to you. I…" he bit his lip and stared off to the side of her head, "that night, when I told you about the New York job offer, I was going to ask you to marry me." He looked back at her, the truth, and his pain, apparent in his eyes.

She yanked her hands from his and clapped them to her face. "What?" The bottom dropped out of her stomach, and she was glad she had the worksurface behind her to hold her up. She stared at Luke in disbelief. "I… you know, I had a *feeling* something was up, but then you told me about New York, and—"

"Everything went to shit," he put in wryly.

"Well, yeah." She gripped the edge of the worktop. "To say the least." Hot tears sprang to her eyes. The perfect wedding she'd dreamt of, the idyllic honeymoon, eventual babies… she could have had it all, everything she'd wanted, if only she hadn't been such a fucking wimp. If only she'd been brave enough to go with him. Hadn't been so stubborn, so determined to make her way in a career she'd ended up ditching anyway. Ugh, what a waste.

She edged past Luke and took a seat at the table, then dropped her head into her hands. Her brain was crowded with thoughts of what could have been, the pain of losing him tearing through her afresh—somehow made worse by the knowledge none of it had needed to happen. And it was all her fault.

After a few moments of mentally castigating herself for being a colossal twat, she became distracted by the sound of movement, followed by the dual taps of mugs being placed on the table, then the scrape of chair legs on the lino floor. Another noise she couldn't quite place—a rustle, perhaps—finally intrigued her enough to make her look up. Next to her cup of tea sat an unopened packet of chocolate digestives—her absolute favourite biscuits.

She flicked her gaze to Luke, who was eyeing her tentatively. She gave him a watery smile, sniffed, and wiped her eyes. "Thank you. For the tea *and* the biscuits."

One side of his mouth flicked up in a lopsided smile. "Not a problem. I brought them as bribery in case you wouldn't let me in."

"I'm surprised you even *wanted* to come in. Surprised you want anything to do with me at all, after I was so stupid and fucking immature," she said bitterly, then hiccupped around a sob. "We could have had *everything*, Luke. Can you ever forgive me?"

"Ro," he used the shortened version of her name only he had ever been allowed to get away with, "there's nothing to forgive. Honestly." He reached across the table and took her hand. "It was a tricky situation. Awkward timing. I'm not saying if I could turn back the clock and do that night over again knowing what I know now, I'd behave exactly the same way, but, well, I've thought about this a lot over the years. God, have I thought about it a lot." He rolled his eyes at the ceiling. "But I finally came to the conclusion it probably wasn't the right thing for us at the time. You didn't want to come to New York, and while I desperately wanted you to, I had no intention of pressuring you into it, because that would have risked causing you to resent me for it. And that might have caused us to split eventually anyway. It's why I didn't propose first, too, because that would have added more pressure to the situation."

He shrugged. "It hurt. A hell of a lot. But things happen for a reason."

"Ugh, all right, king of the clichés."

"Oi," he squeezed her hand and gave her a mock glare, "you're forgetting something—clichés are clichés because they're often true."

Instinctively, she opened her mouth to disagree, until she realised he was right and closed it again. "Fair enough." As she contemplated what he'd said, she came to the conclusion he was probably spot on about it not being the right thing for them at the time. But was it right for them now? There was probably only one way to find out.

Rosie grabbed the packet of biscuits, opened it and removed two, before sliding the packet over to Luke. She dipped one in her tea and munched on it, enjoying the mixture of sweet and savoury that melted over her tongue. Not wanting to linger any more on the difficult conversation they'd just had, she changed the subject. "So, what do you think to the shop?"

If Luke was surprised at the new topic, he didn't show it. Maybe he needed to give his brain and emotions a rest for a while, too. He pulled out two biscuits, placed one next to his mug, and kept hold of the other one. "Well, I only got a quick glimpse, but it looks great. Such a variety of products. Obviously it's now completely the wrong time of year, but I feel like you could come in here and do your entire Christmas present shop in one fell swoop."

"You could always start early. Maybe even grab a bargain or two in the sale. That's what some people do." She dipped her biscuit again and took another bite.

Luke's eyebrows jumped up his forehead. "Seriously? People start next year's Christmas shopping in the post-Christmas sales?"

She nodded as she chewed and swallowed her mouthful. "Why not? You get way more for your money. And it means you spread the cost, rather than dropping loads of money all at once in November and December. It's great for people on a tight budget."

"Hmm, I see that. But knowing me, I'd forget all about what I'd bought and who it was for, forget where I'd stashed it, and buy something else anyway."

"Probably. Or you'd end up finding it after you'd already bought something else, and the recipient would end up with more than one gift."

He chuckled. "Sounds like something I'd do. Speaking of Christmas gifts, did you open yours yesterday evening in the end?" He copied her actions with his biscuit, closing his eyes briefly as he enjoyed it.

Now at a safe distance from their previous topic, they dished the dirt on their respective gifts given and received as they consumed their tea and biscuits.

They were still chatting away when they finished, and Rosie

reluctantly got to her feet. "Sorry to be a killjoy, but we agreed we'd take our time over one cup of tea, and we have. We should crack on now, or I'll still be here at midnight."

He got up, too. "Absolutely. You were a trooper for me yesterday, so it's time to return the favour. Just point me in the right direction and tell me what to do."

"I didn't do it for you," she said, walking around to his side of the table on her way to the door, "I did it for the guests. They deserved a nice Christmas lunch."

He grabbed her wrist before she could pass him. "I'm well aware of that, Rosie. And your kindness is one of the many reasons I love you so much."

She gaped at him, her pulse thrumming in her ears. He… *loved her?* He'd said he still had strong feelings for her, but love? Her nerves getting the better of her and causing her to blab inconsequential nonsense rather than respond to what he'd actually said, she replied, "I-I'm just saying, there's no favour to return. I didn't even know you were going to be there, did I? So if anything, you helping me today means I'll owe *you* a favour—"

He silenced her with a finger to her lips. "Rosie," he growled, glowering at her from beneath a lowered brow, "stop talking about bloody favours, will you? I'm here because I want to be, because I'd do anything for you, and if that also means I get to spend time with you, all the better." He removed his finger from her lips, only to cup her cheek and lean in for a kiss.

After releasing her wrist from his grip, she clung to Luke's upper arms, giving herself over to the kiss she'd been fantasising about since… well, the last one. She'd been on one hell of a rollercoaster of emotion over the last day or so, but one thing was for certain.

She still loved him, too.

Chapter Twelve

Their kiss on the market square bench the previous afternoon had been incredible, if unexpected. Romantic, too—particularly when it'd started snowing. But this one was entirely different. Less of a reunion, more the beginning of something. What that something would turn out to be, she had no idea, but she was too lost in the moment to give it any further thought. With Luke's arms wrapped around her, hauling her against his big, hard body, his beard tickling and scraping her face, his hot tongue exploring her mouth, that familiar aftershave wafting evocatively into her nostrils, she was a mass of dizzying, lustful sensation. Every cell in her yearned for him, ached to have him inside her, making love to her like he used to.

But *would* it be like it used to? His kisses felt both familiar and brand new, somehow—would sex be the same? And should she even be *thinking* about having sex with him? Granted, it wasn't as if they'd only just met, but their shared past was messy, complicated. Painful. At this stage, maybe screwing a stranger was more sensible than jumping back into bed with Luke Adams. Ugh, how had she gone from not being able to think about anything to overthinking everything?

Seeming to pick up on her hesitation, Luke broke the kiss and took a step back, his hands resting lightly on her hips and questions in his eyes. "Are you all right? Do you want to stop? I'm sorry, I—"

She blew out a breath and shook her head. "No, no, I don't want to stop. I'm fine. That was *hot.* Mind-blowingly so. It's just…"

she scrunched up her nose and pointed between the two of them, "there's a lot of baggage, isn't there? And... my brain got involved. You know how it can be."

Luke grinned. "I do. That bloody brain of yours." He gently tapped her temple and scolded the organ in question. "Why'd you have to stick your oar in, huh? We were having a lot of fun." He swept his hand over her skull, smoothing loose wisps of her hair back towards her ponytail as his eyes burned into hers. "Would you like to have some *more* fun? Perhaps with less brain involvement? Stow the baggage away for a while?" He paused, lifted an eyebrow, then murmured, "Do you remember your safe word?"

A bolt of arousal hit her square between the legs, and her heart rate increased. "Y-yes," she said, her voice barely audible even to her own ears. She cleared her throat, then spoke louder. "I-I mean, yes, Sir, I would like to have some more fun. And yes, I remember my safe word."

His grin turned wicked, his eyes darkened, and he gave a single nod. "Good girl. That's what I like to hear. Now, just one more question before we begin: are you on birth control?"

"Yes, Sir." Even as the physical sensations within her ramped up, her mind was quietening. Just like it always did when they dropped into a scene—as Luke well knew.

"Excellent. God knows I'd love for you to have my babies, but all in good time. Now..." He raked his gaze the length of her body, sizing her up, making decisions. Perhaps after a decade of being apart, he didn't know where to begin. "Take off your jumper, and whatever top you have underneath it. Leave your bra."

She quickly did as he asked, habit and previous expected etiquette dictating she folded the removed clothes and placed them neatly on a chair. Then she stood, her back to the table they'd just vacated, waiting.

A deep rumble of approval issued from Luke's chest. "Christ, Rosie. The years have been good to you. That skin, those curves. And, of course, my personal favourite," he stepped forward and cupped her breasts over her bra, "those luscious tits of yours. Are they bigger?"

"Yes, Sir." Her respectfully lowered gaze meant she was staring directly at his crotch. *Not* so respectful. Arousal flared again as she spotted the impressive erection forming a bulge in his jeans. "Because I'm fatter than I used to be. Some of the weight went to my boobs."

"Rosie," he said sternly, making her heart skip a beat. "Look at me."

She pulled in a breath through her nostrils and obeyed. His pupils were so blown she could barely pick out the colour of his irises.

"I don't want to hear any more comments about you being 'fatter', all right? You look incredible. Healthy, curvy. Fucking beautiful. Incidentally," he slipped his fingers to her nape, his thumb to her throat, and leaned in until his warm breath fanned over her face, "I wouldn't give a shit if you were twice the size. You've always been perfect to me, Rosie, and you always will be. Now, be a good girl and give me a kiss."

She opened her mouth willingly to his rough lips and

possessing tongue, melting into his embrace, into the feeling of him against her, his hard to her soft, the tactile sensation of his woollen jumper against her naked skin. A thick fog of lust filled her head, leaving her with nothing but need, yearning. She submitted to it, as she already had to Luke.

His hands were hot, almost scorching. They were seemingly everywhere at once—in her hair, cupping her face, smoothing over her shoulders, her arms, her hips. Flat against her back and hauling her closer still. She fisted her hands in the hem of his jumper to stop her succumbing to the temptation to slide them underneath the material to touch his flesh.

Their lips and teeth clashed, and their tongues slipped together in an increasingly frantic, erotic dance. Her nipples strained against the fabric of her bra, and the gusset of her knickers grew wetter with every passing minute. Their laboured breaths, pants and moans swirled in the air around them, until Luke eventually pulled away with a grunt.

"Fuck." He ran a hand through his hair, then dropped it to rearrange himself downstairs. "What are you doing to me, Ro?"

Blood pumped so powerfully through her she was hot all over. It was actually making her a tad lightheaded. She leaned on the edge of the table for support. "The same thing you're doing to me, I imagine, Sir."

"Touché," he shot back with a smirk, then drank her in once more. When his gaze returned to her face, he said, "Everything off. I want to see you. All of you."

She wanted to see all of him, too, but opted to keep that

sentiment to herself. With any luck, her nakedness would inspire him to strip off as well, so they could be fully skin to skin. Mentally crossing her fingers that would be the case, she took off her boots, then her socks, followed by her jeans, bra and knickers—stowing each away tidily either on or beneath the same chair as her other stuff.

"My God," Luke breathed as she turned to face him once she was fully nude, then winced and pushed his palm against his raging cock. "You're stunning."

Gazing up at him through her eyelashes as demurely as she could, the way she knew perfectly well drove him crazy, she whispered, "Thank you, Sir. I'm glad I please you."

He gulped and rolled his gaze to the ceiling. She was picking at the edges of his control, and it was fraying. After a beat, he righted his head, then reached back over his shoulder, grabbed a fistful of material and hauled his jumper and T-shirt off in one fell swoop.

She bit her lip as he was revealed to her. God, he was as sexy as ever. Marginally thicker, marginally softer, but in a natural way which suited him. A couple of unfamiliar scars marred his forearms—occupational hazards, she guessed.

He caught her eye as he went for his belt, then playfully jammed his hands onto his hips. "You like what you see?" he asked, wiggling his eyebrows.

Rosie couldn't help the snort of laughter that escaped her. Pushing through her mirth, she replied with feigned flippancy, "I couldn't possibly say, Sir. Not without seeing *everything*."

"Minx." He pursed his lips, then bent over and undid his bootlaces, allowing Rosie a glorious view of his shoulders and upper back as he did so, the muscles flexing deliciously with his movements.

She quickly averted her gaze as he straightened, toed off the boots, then hooked off his socks, before returning his attention to his belt. The leather snapped as he flipped it open—deliberately, she thought—sending echoes of erotic awareness crashing through her. Thoughts of the countless times he'd whacked her arse with a leather belt caused juice to seep from her pussy and soak her inner thighs. She clenched them together, hoping he wouldn't notice.

No such luck. His hands stilled, the ends of his belt hanging loose, and his expression fell into harsh lines. "Rosie, are you trying to get off?"

"N-no, Sir. Never without your permission. Just in need of a little… relief."

His eyebrows leapt up. "Relief, you say? No… I think I know what you need, beautiful. One moment." In a series of swift, efficient movements, he rendered himself naked—bar his boxers, which were black, fitted, and bulged even more at the crotch than his jeans had, owing to the thinner material.

"Turn around," he commanded. "Hands on the table, feet shoulder-width apart, arse pointing towards me."

Swallowing hard, she complied. She had an idea of what was going to happen next, but wouldn't swear to anything specific. Luke was nothing if not inventive—and surprising.

Luke let out a hiss. "Still the best arse I've ever seen." He ran a finger down the centre of her right buttock, then her left. He pushed his fingertip hard into the fleshiest part of her left buttock before removing it. "Bit pale, though. Needs some colour, in my opinion."

Rosie's stomach somersaulted, and she pressed her lips together. And just *how* did he plan to give it that colour?

Mercifully, she didn't have to wait long to find out. Luke smoothed his big hands over her backside, then squeezed, hard.

She yelped, unused to the sensation after such a long time. The pinch of discomfort soon melded into warmth, into pleasure, and the heaviness, the *neediness* between her thighs increased. At this rate, he'd be able to smell her arousal as well as see it.

Luke chuckled and repeated his movements, adopting what was almost a kneading action—one she knew was designed to get her blood flowing, in order to prepare her for what he planned to do next. She locked her knees and hips, determined not to push her arse further towards him and give away just how desperate she was for him to do something, *anything,* but mostly to make her come. That'd just make him torment her all the more.

Her patience and determination paid off when, after a couple more minutes of manipulating her flesh, he drew his hands away, only to land one of them on her right buttock with a *thwack.* There was barely a pause before the same hand thwacked her other cheek. She gasped, then moaned as the stinging pain deepened into pleasure.

"Good girl," Luke purred, stroking her bottom. "You've always taken a spanking well, my love, haven't you?"

"T-thank you, Sir," she replied, internally basking in his praise and eager to earn more, "I-I try."

His response was to spank her again, right then left in quick succession. Her pussy throbbed and seeped more juices, but she did little more than gasp. With her thighs spread the way they were—a deliberate action on Luke's part, she suspected, designed to stop her squeezing them together—it was entirely possible her natural lubrication would succumb to gravity and make its way to the lino between her feet.

Spank, spank. Right, left.

Spank, spank. Left, right this time. Changing things up. Keeping her on her toes.

And again.

Then again.

Over and over, a rhythmic action, each blow landing on a slightly different area of her bum, so the heat spread and melded until her entire arse felt white-hot, her knees weak, and her clit the size of a grape. Only her determination to please kept her in place, kept her from begging—silently or otherwise—Luke to fuck her. Plus, she knew from experience it was better if she waited for *him* to be the one to break, rather than her.

Finally, he stopped. Bar the sound of their breathing, the silence was deafening, and she fancied she could hear sizzling from her arse cheeks.

Luke let out a deep, abandoned groan. "Christ, Rosie. You took that like an absolute fucking champ." Knowing he couldn't see her face, she allowed herself a grin. *Result!* "Your arse looks *incredible.* And I'm absolutely fucking rock-hard. I-I have to be inside you. Immediately."

There came the rustle of movement, the lightest of *thwumps*—presumably his boxers dropping to the floor—then the gentle caress of hands on her bum, followed by the brush of knuckles against her crease. Finally, *finally,* he began feeding his cock into her.

Luke hissed. "Oh. My. Fucking. God. You are *drenched.* And red-hot. Tight. Uhhhh. At this rate, I'll come in thirty seconds, like a fucking horny teenager."

"Ahhhh." Rosie closed her eyes and tossed her head back as her pussy stretched wide around Luke's long, thick shaft. By the time he bottomed out, his ballsac pressed tightly up against her vulva, she was already teetering on the edge of climax. The D/s play, combined with the spanking, had heightened the already extremely pleasurable sensations filling her body, and she found herself hoping Luke would take pity on her poor, neglected clitoris—particularly if he was genuinely worried he wasn't going to last long himself.

Luke gave a sharp jerk of his hips, making them both cry out, then draped himself over her back, the delicious heat of his bare skin against hers adding more fuel to her fire. He placed one large hand next to hers on the table, bracing himself, and slipped the other around to her front. He stroked and rubbed her swollen labia, thoroughly exploring the point at which their bodies joined, before zeroing in on her clit. *Yesssss.*

"Ahhh," he breathed into her ear, slowly easing himself out of her, before forging back in, all the while circling that needy bundle of nerve endings. "Rosie, this is perfection. I've missed this so much. Missed you." He rocked in and out of her, slow and deep, sending sparks of pleasure dancing across her skin.

"I've missed you too, Luke," she murmured, then inhaled sharply as he began kissing and nibbling her neck. "Oh God, that's good." The kissing, the fucking, the talented, determined fingers on her clit combined with the latent burn in her backside to push her relentlessly towards orgasm.

Luke grunted as her core clenched around him. "Fucking *hell*, Rosie." He picked up the speed of his thrusts, as well as his movements on her clit. "Do that again and I'll blow."

She smirked to herself, then let out a cry as the pressure within her began to reach breaking point. "Sir, I really need to come… may I?"

He nipped her shoulder, then murmured into her ear, "You'd fucking better, beautiful."

With permission came release. Sweet, sweet release. She threw her head back and yelled her ecstasy at the ceiling, as her orgasm tore through her with a ferocity she'd forgotten she could experience. Her internal walls undulated powerfully around Luke's cock, and within seconds his climax followed her own.

They jerked and spasmed and gasped and swore together, like they had so many times before. And in Luke's arms, Rosie felt like she was exactly where she was supposed to be. Where she should have been all along. She only wished she could see his face, which was currently buried in the crook of her neck and shoulder as he rode out his orgasm.

After a minute or two they disentangled, moving about on legs as unsteady as a newborn alpaca's and exchanging pleased, post-orgasmic grins.

"Are you all right?" Luke asked as he stepped into his boxers. "I wasn't too hard with the spanking? Or… anything else?"

Rosie shook her head as she retrieved her undies from the chair and put them on, stifling a wince as the material brushed over her tormented bottom. "No. It was amazing. All of it. Absolutely incredible. Trouble is," she glanced at her watch, then gave him a wry look, "I'm even further behind with my work now."

Luke had the good grace to appear chagrined. "Yeah… sorry about that. I promise that wasn't what I had in mind when I said we should take our time over a cup of tea." He grabbed his T-shirt and slipped it on. "I could do with another one now, after that. I'm fucking wiped."

Rosie fixed him with a stern glance, despite the happy hormones whizzing through her system. "Get dressed, and we'll talk about *maybe* having more tea. Maybe." Who was she kidding? All she wanted to do right now was curl up and have a lovely post-shag snooze. But she had way too much work to do, so another shot of caffeine was absolutely on the table. Wouldn't hurt to make him wait for it, though.

He began dragging on his clothes at a rapid rate, which both amused Rosie *and* made her sad. He looked great naked, and she'd been very much enjoying the view.

Only when they were fully clothed did she gather up their mugs and move over to flip on the kettle. "We're taking this one into the shop with us, though. We're going to work and drink, okay?"

Chapter Thirteen

Rosie had to give Luke his due—after their impromptu shag, he did make good on his promise to help her out. They'd taken their second cup of tea and the chocolate digestives into the shop, and they'd knuckled down, sipping, nibbling and chatting as they worked.

By the time he declared he had to leave, his expression and tone full of regret, the packet of biscuits was seriously depleted and she actually didn't have much more to do. Just a handful more markdowns, one crate of new stock to go out, then a general check over to make sure everything was clean and tidy ready for the following day's customers.

"Thanks for the help today. I really appreciate it."

"You're very welcome," he replied, heading for the staff room to collect his coat, hat and snood. When he returned with them, he added, "I have to admit, it's not quite how I expected to spend my Boxing Day, but it's certainly been… fun." A glint in his eye made it clear which part he'd found *particularly* fun. Not that she could blame him. He pulled his snood over his head, and when his face reappeared on the other side of it, he was flashing her a wide grin. He jammed his hat on over his dark hair, then shrugged into his coat and zipped it up.

She couldn't help grinning back as she retrieved the keys and led him to the door. "Do you think your shift at work will be as fun?"

"Absolutely not," he replied, stepping up beside her, his

expression still full of amusement. "I can't imagine I will be commanding any of my colleagues to strip off, bend over a table, then spanking their arse and fucking them until my world is rocked. It's not usually how things go over there."

"No?" She smirked as she inserted the key into the lock and turned it. It was dark outside now, and the light from the shop glowed almost eerily off the snow. "Not that kind of place?"

"No. Much more cooking than fucking going on."

"Probably better for customer relations."

"Oh yeah, 'cause that's the *only* reason." He rolled his eyes.

Rosie snickered. "Well, I hope it goes okay, and I'll see you when I see you."

A flicker of doubt crossed Luke's face, but was quickly replaced with a smile. He put his hand on the door handle. "Thank you. Make sure you lock up behind me again, won't you?"

"Will do."

He leaned down and kissed her cheek, his lips warm against her skin. "Bye then." He opened the door and stepped out.

"Bye. Safe travels."

He closed the door, then stood on the other side of it and waved, before blowing her a kiss. She mirrored the gesture, and they gazed into each other's eyes for a moment, before he turned and strode off down the street.

She watched him until he went out of sight, then locked the door and pushed the button to drop the shutters over the windows and door. There was nobody out there, but it still felt weird being in the shop, all the lights on, like she was in a goldfish bowl.

After pocketing the keys, she turned her attention to her remaining tasks. It was plenty warm enough in the building, but she was still very much looking forward to heading home for a nice hot shower—while somehow avoiding aiming the spray at her tender backside—getting into her snuggly pyjamas, then making something delicious for dinner, which she'd eat on a tray on her lap, in front of the TV. A nice, relaxing evening to wind down, before what would hopefully be a busy day tomorrow.

As she applied yellow sale stickers to a bunch of cute Christmas earrings, her mind inevitably wandered back to Luke. Hardly a surprise when her entire body was still feeling the aftereffects of what had taken place between them. A dull throb in her buttocks, a delicious ache between her legs, and… confusion in her brain. The temporary quiet her submission to Luke had elicited in her mind had been delicious, but now the noise was filtering back in.

She couldn't quite put her finger on what exactly was causing the confusion, though. He'd said he still loved her, and she sure as shit still loved him. They were both available, and the sex had been as incredible as ever. Maybe more so. Yes, there was baggage, a past, but from what she'd gleaned so far, they were on the same page these days. Neither of them had any intentions of leaving their jobs to move halfway across the world, they both wanted marriage and kids… so what was the problem? It seemed they were more compatible than ever.

Trouble was, this had all come completely out of the blue. On Christmas Eve, her biggest issue had been finding out her parents were poorly and making a quick change of her plans for Christmas Day as a result.

Now, a mere two days later, she was dealing with the sudden and unexpected reappearance of the love of her life. A man she hadn't seen or heard from in ten years. A man she'd thought lived in New York City, and worked in some swanky restaurant. He might as well have been a million miles away, for all he'd factored into her life. But now he was here, seemed keen to reconcile, or at least to discuss it, and Rosie was struggling to wrap her head around it all. Their kisses and that amazing shag had only added to the confusion.

Her life was great now. Yes, things had been tricky when she and Luke had split, then when she'd decided to switch career paths, but things had been settled for so long. Barring James and his wife and kids heading off for a wonderful new life in Australia earlier in the year, everything in Rosie Kilbride's world had been quiet, comfortable. Her mum and dad were good, she was good, she loved running her little business empire, and honestly hadn't given much thought to romance or relationships for a while. She'd been too busy. Thanks to the contents of her bedside table, she hadn't even bothered about sex, either.

Did she really want to rock the nice, steady boat that was her life, for the sake of rekindling a relationship that had imploded in spectacular fashion a decade ago? Yes, they were different people now—older, more mature—but who was to say it wouldn't all go tits up again? Just because they were getting along at the moment, and the attraction was as potent as ever, the sex as scorching, it didn't mean things were guaranteed to work out. Could she really risk putting herself through that agony again?

And Luke had so recently been through some major life changes—the loss of his lovely mum and the sudden move back to the UK and all that entailed. While he seemed okay on the surface, who was to say how fragile he was—understandably—feeling underneath it all? Was it really fair to risk piling more emotional turmoil onto him?

She sighed, then found her phone and put her music back on. Loud, in an attempt to distract her from her incessant, annoying wonderings. She needed to finish what she was doing and get out of here, otherwise, despite Luke's help, she'd still end up staying way too late.

After taking a couple of deep breaths to calm and centre herself, she jumped in to singing along, letting the song, the music, the lyrics, fill her consciousness, leaving just enough processing power in her brain for her to crack on with her re-pricing.

Thankfully, the forced brain reboot worked, and she had everything done within an hour. The shop looked a little bare without all its glorious festive decorations, but that was always the case post-Christmas. She'd feel the same about the house when she finally got around to taking everything down there, too. A friend had told her that in Iceland, they left their Christmas lights up through January and even into February to help counteract the long, dark nights and gloomy days. It was one hell of a good idea, in Rosie's opinion. Anything to keep mood and morale up in the winter was a bonus. It was bad enough in the middle of England—in Iceland, so far north and with much less daylight, it had to be way worse.

Back in the staff room, she washed up the mugs and spoon she and Luke had used, dried and put them away, then grabbed some cleaning spray and a cloth, and gave the worktop and table a good wipe down. Her mind tried to lure her back into thinking of what had taken place in that very spot earlier, but she resisted. Straightened the chairs, turned all the lights off and scurried out of there.

By now she was tired and hungry, and the call of home was strong. She bundled into her coat, scarf and hat, completed all of her safety and security checks, grabbed her stuff, killed the music, heating and lights, and let herself out into the bitterly cold evening. She gasped at the sting of the freezing air against her skin.

She made her way to her car, carefully treading in the fresh snow, rather than going over hers and Luke's earlier tracks, hoping for better traction. After a slightly hairy moment in which her foot broke through the layer of snow to a manhole cover, which was slippery and almost had her tumbling over, she reached her car with no further issues. The car park and main roads were okay, but, as she'd expected, the housing estate she lived on was somewhat of a shitshow. The council did absolutely nothing to clear or grit the roads or pavements, instead providing poorly-situated grit bins and expecting residents to collect and spread it themselves—if there was even any grit put in said bins following previous spells of snowy or icy weather which had depleted the stocks.

As a result, the folks living on the estate—herself included—tended to adopt a hope-for-the-best method. Just hit the accelerator and pray the tyres gained enough purchase to get you where you needed to go. That was all well and good on fresh snow—albeit still inadvisable—but now there'd been a day's worth of people coming and going, it was compacted, and the dropping temperature meant ice skates would be preferable to tyres.

Rosie pulled on to her drive in one piece, with her steering wheel in a death grip, then jumped when her phone pinged. She parked, put the handbrake on, then heaved a sigh of relief as she switched off the engine. Deciding to allow herself a moment of respite before stepping out onto yet another potentially slippery surface, she retrieved her phone from her pocket.

It was a text from Luke. *Please let me know when you're home safe. Luke xxx*

She smiled and instinctively went to reply, then frowned and paused with her thumb hovering over the phone's keyboard. He was just being considerate, sweet, but was it a good idea to respond? It didn't seem fair to lead him on, give him false hope, if she ultimately decided them getting back together wasn't what she wanted. *Perhaps you should have thought of that before you had sex with him again.*

Sighing, she locked the phone's screen and shoved the device in her pocket, then grabbed her bag and keys and exited the car. She locked it, then gingerly stepped up her pathway to the door. Only her earlier footprints, and those of a particularly hardy cat marred the snow's surface, so she made it inside without too much trouble. If the snow was still around tomorrow, she'd make the time to shovel it from her path and drive before she headed out.

Safely inside, she deactivated the security alarm, locked her front door, hung up the keys, then took off her outerwear and put each item in its correct place. The entire time, the phone still residing in her coat pocket seemed to call to her. She itched to respond to Luke's message, as much out of a sense of politeness than because she wanted to speak to him, even if only by text.

Maybe just a polite, casual response would be okay? He'd enquired after her safety—it seemed only right to let him know she was home, so he wouldn't worry. But then where would *that* lead? A quid pro quo? Goodnight messages? Good morning messages? When can I see you again messages?

It felt like a slippery slope to Rosie, so she held firm, and threw herself into her relaxing evening. It was considerably less relaxing than it *should* have been, because out of necessity she'd had to throw in a whole bunch of distractions to stop her obsessing over Luke's text and whether she should respond to it or not. Even putting her phone on silent, turning off the vibrate function, and placing it face down on the coffee table didn't help much—it was still there as a visual reminder of her inner turmoil.

As a result, by the time she settled into bed, she was physically and mentally exhausted. Unfortunately, before she could drift off to sleep, her troublesome brain jumped right back to the unanswered text message, leaving Rosie to go over and over her thought processes and decisions, back and forth on the whole damn thing, until she finally lost consciousness, the paleness of her bedroom ceiling imprinted on her vision.

Chapter Fourteen

The 27th dawned dry and sunny, and an overnight temperature increase meant Rosie's planned driveway shovelling session wasn't needed—much to her delight. It was a glorious winter morning, and only small piles of snow remained, dotted here and there on the pavements and roads, where it had been compacted, pushed aside by tyres, or shovelled there by residents. A sad-looking, rapidly-shrinking snowman held court in the middle of a front lawn a few doors up from Rosie's house. She doubted it would be much more than a tiny hump topped with a carrot, a bunch of pebbles and a woollen scarf by the time she arrived home again that evening. At least the kids had had fun while they could, particularly since having enough snow to make a snowman was a rarity in these parts.

Bar squinting against the bright sunlight, which also reflected off the damp roads—she hadn't had time to go back into the house in search of her sunglasses—Rosie's journey to work was a breeze, the main roads completely clear of snow and ice. In contrast was the car park behind the shop. Thanks to the lack of sunlight reaching the tiny space, it still held on to a thin layer of snow, making driving, parking, and walking tricky, but achievable, meaning she once again reached her destination unscathed.

Which was just as well, since from the moment she arrived at the shop to the moment she left, her day was hectic. Catching up with her staff members and stockists, serving customers, keeping on top of paperwork, updating the shop's social media accounts, answering queries by phone, email and direct message, restocking the shelves… it was such a whirlwind that by the time she collapsed, hair still damp from the shower, into bed that night, not even her overactive brain could keep her awake.

The following day was Saturday, which promised to be busier still. Knowing from experience customer numbers would be at their highest from mid-morning to lunchtime, Rosie opened the shop at the designated time of 9 a.m., then left her colleague, Louise, in charge while she nipped to Ingrid's café to grab a couple of takeaway posh lattes. Maybe she'd treat herself and Louise to a slice of cake each as well—a delicious sugar rush to help them get through the day.

Hunched inside her coat, a woolly hat pulled down over her ears, she headed along the high street, waving to and smiling at the fellow shopkeepers she passed. The scene felt very Christmassy, since the town's festive lights and decorations were still up, and would be into the new year—though not for nearly as long as in Iceland, and the lights probably wouldn't be switched on when it grew dark.

As she walked along the street, with its occasional piles of remaining snow, she couldn't help wondering that she hadn't already heard from Ingrid, who had to be positively champing at the bit for her promised dose of gossip. But then, she'd mentioned she planned to deep clean the café before reopening after Christmas, so she'd likely been just as busy over the past couple of days as Rosie had.

When Rosie pushed open the café door, the warmth and the scent of coffee hit her instantly. Like The Creative Collective, the place looked a little bare without all its Christmas decorations, but was still as welcoming as ever. The tinkle of the bell over the door drew the attention of Ingrid, who looked to be juggling multiple drink orders behind the counter. Despite her obvious preoccupation, she flashed Rosie a huge smile. "Hiya. Be with you in just a sec."

"No worries. Whenever you're ready."

Within a minute or two, Ingrid had placed the drinks she'd made onto a tray and whizzed them over to the relevant customers. When she returned, she asked, "Okay, what can I get you, sweetie?"

"Two salted caramel lattes, and," she indicated the goodie-packed display case she'd thoroughly perused while waiting for Ingrid to come back, "one rocky road, and one slice of Victoria sponge, please. To take away." She placed hers and Louise's reusable cups on the counter with a smile.

"Uh, no." Ingrid grabbed the reusable cups and placed them by the coffee machine, then shook her head and wagged her index finger. "Absolutely not. You, young lady, are going to sit your pert little bottom in one of the chairs at *that* table," she indicated a spot in a corner, "and I will join you in just a moment for a nice chat. Which cake was yours? Would you like that now, or to take away?"

Rosie blinked, steamrollered by Ingrid's insistence— although, of course, not at all surprised. Her friend was quite the force of nature. "Both cakes to take away, please." She figured she'd have hers as a late-morning snack, since there was a good chance there wouldn't be time for lunch.

"No problem. Now shoo, go and grab that table before anyone else does. I'm going to let Stacey know I need her to take over for a bit."

Shaking her head, Rosie turned and did as she'd been commanded. She hung her coat on the back of her chair, sat, and placed her bag beside her feet. After removing her hat, she balanced it on top of her bag before surreptitiously smoothing down her hair. Then, not wanting to look at her phone—which by now held quite a few unanswered messages from Luke—she idly people-watched, both others in the café and those wandering by the window, going about their business. It was still relatively quiet out on the high street, so she wasn't worried about Louise being mobbed by customers in her absence—though she could always use that as an excuse if Ingrid's questioning became too intrusive.

"So," came her friend's voice, making Rosie snap her attention away from the window and back to her immediate surroundings, "are you going to fill me in, then?"

Rosie wrapped her hands around the glass mug Ingrid had placed in front of her, then stared into its steamy depths, enjoying the sweet scent drifting up her nostrils. She contemplated playing dumb, but all that would do was delay the inevitable. "W-what do you want to know?"

"Are you kidding?" Ingrid replied, screwing up her face. "*Everything,* sweetie. Absolutely everything. It was so weird to find out my very old school friend and my fairly new friend used to be in a relationship. But the more I thought about it, the more I figured you were perfectly suited. So what happened? Back in the day, I mean." She blew on the surface of her drink, then raised her eyebrows at Rosie in query.

"It was a long time ago. Ten years. We'd been together around two years when it all went wrong." She sucked in a breath, then sighed it out. "It was all to do with Luke's New York restaurant job. Things between us were going great, then he got the offer and asked me to go with him. I didn't want to go. I was at an early stage in my journalism career and didn't want to risk losing any momentum and ruining things for myself. But it was an incredible opportunity for him, so I encouraged him to take it. Obviously, he did. And… that was that, really." She shrugged, not wanting to go into any further detail, particularly when it came to how crushed she'd been. "I was pretty damn surprised to see him standing in your kitchen the other day. Far as I was concerned, he was still in New York. We hadn't spoken since that day I left his place after telling him to go without me."

Ingrid took a sip of her drink, then nodded and said softly, "You, er, know why he's back now, don't you?"

Rosie bobbed her head, a sudden lump appearing in her throat. She forcefully swallowed it down. "H-his mum. He told me what happened. Horrendous. And so unfair. I always got on with Cathy so well. She was lovely."

"She was," Ingrid agreed with a sad smile. "I have incredibly fond memories of her from when Luke and I were kids. We were in the same friendship group, so our paths crossed quite a bit. She was always nice—and she spoiled us lot rotten. Gave us extra sweets, biscuits, and pop, and made us promise not to tell our parents."

"Yeah." Rosie chuckled. "That sounds like her. John's great, too. Luke says he's coping quite well, all things considered." She blew on her latte, then drank some. The flavours exploded over her tongue, making her hum with delight.

"Can't have been easy for either of them. Especially with it being so sudden, and Luke being so far away at the time. But at least he's here now…" There was a strange emphasis on Ingrid's last sentence, and Rosie looked over to see the older woman staring at her meaningfully.

"What?" Rosie asked, wide-eyed. "Why are you giving me that face?"

Ingrid shot her a filthy look. "Don't you be coy with me, Rosie Kilbride. As awful as what happened to poor Cathy is, and how devastating it's been for John and Luke, that's not what I want to know about. From what I can tell, you were the perfect, loved-up couple, and you broke up more due to circumstances than any lack of feelings. But now the universe has brought you back together, and you clearly still have the hots for each other… so what's going on? What happened on Christmas Day? One minute we were all enjoying a nice dinner, the next you freaked out, took off, and Luke grabbed both your coats and went after you. You were gone a while, too, then you came back here all smiley and hung out to finish your meals. I have to say, it was a bit of a mind-fuck."

After enjoying another delicious mouthful of her latte, Rosie said, "I… never wanted to break up with Luke." She glanced around to make sure no one was paying them any attention, and lowered her voice. Heat flared into her cheeks as she forced out the confession she'd been so reluctant to make. "It wasn't just the job thing that held me back. I-I wasn't *brave* enough to go with him. I loved him with all my heart, but I just couldn't do it. I was young, only twenty-two. I blamed him for going anyway, even though I'd told him to. I've never clicked with someone the same way since. He was—still is—the love of my life. Our split broke my heart." She swallowed and cast her gaze to the ceiling, hoping talking about it wouldn't cause the same reaction as when it had happened. She'd already had enough embarrassment. "On Christmas Day, when a certain song came on, it triggered a memory. Of when Luke and I first said 'I love you' to each other. Obviously I've heard that song a bazillion times over the years and it's been okay. It was awful at first, but I hardened myself to it over time. But having been in close proximity to him all day, and dealing with the emotions that stirred up in me, well, the song was the last straw. I just had to get out of there."

"Oh, sweetie." Ingrid placed her hand on Rosie's and gave it a squeeze. "I'm so sorry. That must have been horrible. But you obviously," she paused, clearly casting around for the right wording, "talked, when he went after you? Sorted things out? You seemed happy enough when you came back here, so I figured everything was okay." She gasped as something occurred to her. "Everything *was* okay, wasn't it? You'd tell me if it wasn't, right? I'll kick his arse if he—"

"No!" Rosie twisted her hand so it was palm up, and grabbed Ingrid's, then held on to it. "No arse kicking necessary, Ingrid. Though your concern is touching, and appreciated. I was upset when I ran out, as you saw, and I didn't really want to talk to Luke—or anyone else, for that matter—at that point. But we *did* talk, and, aside from finding out about Cathy—though I'd guessed something was amiss when I learnt John was at the meal—it turned out to be a good thing. We got lots of things out in the open, cleared the air. Dealt with stuff that had been festering for a decade."

Ingrid quirked an eyebrow. "And?"

"And what?"

"Oh, come on! I wasn't born yesterday. The vibe between the two of you when you came back here, all pink-cheeked and covered in snow, was one of more than just friends, or ex-lovers." She paused, a smirk twitching at her lips. "It was electric, actually. I found myself sanitising the tables extra thoroughly when I did my deep clean, as I couldn't help wondering whether the two of you had been at it in here."

"Ingrid!" Rosie's eyes almost popped clean out of her head.

"What? You're clearly still attracted to each other, it was Christmas, emotions were running high. I wouldn't blame you for rekindling an old flame—even if it was in my café." She wiggled her eyebrows theatrically while treating her to a huge grin.

"Well, we didn't. Not in your café, not anywhere. We finished our food, chatted, cleared everything away, locked up, then Luke walked me to my car and we went our separate ways."

"Hmm. Well, that tracks based on when the keys dropped through my letterbox, but you've seen him since, right? Or at least spoken to him?"

"Yes." She took another sip of her latte.

Ingrid gave her a wry look. "Have I got to drag this out of you word by bloody word?"

"Christ, you're nosey."

"Well, that's the pot calling the kettle black, isn't it? When have you *ever* let me keep something to myself? You're like a dog with a bone. You won't let anything go. Your journalistic training, I assume. Far as I'm concerned, I'm just getting my own back."

Rosie tutted. "Touché. All right, all right. Like I said, we parted ways on Christmas Night. I went home, he went back to his dad's. It was snowing quite a lot by that point, and I was preoccupied with getting home safely, so I didn't think about the fact we should have exchanged contact details until it was too late—since I deleted his contact details when we broke up, and my number is different to the one I had when we were together. But I wasn't too worried, because I knew I could easily get his number from you."

"You didn't, though," Ingrid said, frowning.

"I didn't need to. He showed up at the shop on Boxing Day. He knew I was going to be there, because I'd mentioned it the previous day."

"Oh." Ingrid's eyebrows leapt up, and she gave a small smile. "That's cute. Romantic, too. Heading out in all that snow. The roads were a bloody nightmare—or at least they were first thing. I should know, because I came here to start the deep clean. I was a nervous wreck by the time I arrived." She paused. "I take it you let him in?"

"I did."

Ingrid glared at her.

Rosie tutted again and rolled her eyes. "All right! Bloody hell. Yes, I let him in. We talked some more, had a cup of tea and some biscuits, then he helped me in the shop for a few hours before he had to go to work." Ingrid might be pressing her for details, but she certainly wasn't going to give any on what happened *after* the cup of tea and biscuits.

"Mmm-hmm." The older woman's expression was completely deadpan.

"*Mmm-hmm?* What do you mean, mmm-hmm? You make it sound like you don't believe me."

"Oh, I believe you, sweetie. I just don't think you're telling me the whole story." She narrowed her eyes and assessed her friend. "I think you shagged him."

Rosie opened her mouth to deny it, but let out a sigh instead. There was no point in lying. She'd never been much good at it, and Ingrid had a way of getting information out of her. Perhaps she'd missed her calling and should have been a journalist instead of Rosie. "Well, yes, if you must know, I did."

Ingrid gave a fist pump. "Yes! I knew it. So, are you guys getting back together, then? Or are you back together already?" Her eyes glittered with excitement.

"No, we're not back together," Rosie said, shaking her head. "And we won't be getting back together, either."

"Huh? What am I missing here?" Ingrid's brow wrinkled. "Why the hell not?"

"I… don't think it's the right thing to do. Luke and I aren't the same people any more. We can't pretend nothing ever happened and simply pick up where we left off. It didn't work out ten years ago, and there are no guarantees it'll work out now. I really don't want to put myself through the trauma of another break-up. And

Luke's already been through enough with losing his mum. It's not fair."

"O...kay." If anything, Ingrid looked even more confused than she already had. "But, sweetie, there are never any guarantees in life. Except for death and taxes, as the old saying goes. Surely it's worth the risk if you love each other? He obviously thinks it is, despite the emotional turmoil he must be experiencing since losing his mum. In fact, her dying so young and so suddenly has probably made him even more determined to grab happiness when it's offered and hold on to it with both hands. He showed up at your shop in the bloody snow, after all. I take it he wants to get back together?"

Rosie dropped her gaze to the table, nodding. God, when would this conversation be over? She felt like Ingrid had cracked her chest open like a walnut and was peering at the inner workings of her heart, poking at them until her curiosity was satisfied.

"So..." Ingrid prodded. "How did you leave things?"

She picked up her drink and took a long, slow draught to buy herself some time. Ingrid wasn't going to like this. Placing it down, she finally responded, "Well, he went off to work, and I haven't seen or spoken to him since."

"But you've exchanged phone numbers?"

"Yes."

"So why haven't you spoken since?"

"Because I've been ignoring his messages," Rosie muttered.

"Sorry? Did you just say you've been ignoring his messages?" Her friend looked as though her head was about to explode.

"Yes. I *told* you, I don't think us getting back together is a good idea. The sex should never have happened."

Ingrid sat back heavily in her chair, her expression sobering. "Okay, well, that's your prerogative. But if part of your reasoning for not giving it a go is that you're concerned about his mental health should things not work out between you, perhaps you should consider how ghosting him might be affecting his mental health."

Rosie frowned and shook her head. "I'm not ghosting him."

"Sweetie, I'm sorry, but that's *exactly* what you're doing. It's bad enough when people do it to someone they hardly know, or have been casually dating. But to do it to someone you claim is the love of your life, someone you say you don't want to risk hurting... well, this is hurting him already, Rosie. I guarantee it. If you don't want things to go any further between the two of you, that's fair enough, but you should at least have the decency to tell him. He's a good guy—he doesn't deserve this. And I think, deep down, you know this already. Right," she finished what was left of her drink, then placed her palms on the table and pushed herself to her feet, "I need to get back to work." As she passed by Rosie's chair, Ingrid placed a hand on Rosie's shoulder and gave it a rub. "I'll get your takeaway order sorted now. Just think about what I said, won't you? After all, how would you feel if the roles were reversed?"

Chapter Fifteen

Rosie passed the rest of the day in somewhat of a daze, unable to stop thinking about her conversation with Ingrid. She was immensely grateful for Louise, who gently ushered her away from the counter after Rosie almost gave a customer more in change than they'd actually handed over in the first place. "I'll take care of the till for the rest of the day, shall I? Why don't you top up some stock or something?"

It wasn't Louise's place to be suggesting what Rosie should be doing, but Rosie recognised she was being about as much use as a chocolate teapot, so she took the friendly sentiment how it was intended and flashed her colleague an appreciative smile before retreating to the relative safety of the stock room.

Thankfully, closing time arrived with no further incidents, and Rosie waved Louise off at 5:32, promising she wouldn't be far behind. After a final check over to make sure the shop was clean and tidy enough for opening again on Monday morning, Rosie closed up and headed for her car. She had to go to the supermarket on her way home, to pick up something quick for her dinner, as well as what she needed for the planned Christmas Day re-do with her parents the following day. After that, though, a quiet, relaxing evening was on the cards.

Perhaps it was because it had been such a lovely, sunny day, but it felt much colder now it was dark, and Rosie was glad of the protection against the bitter evening afforded by her coat, scarf and hat. Her hands were stuffed deeply into her pockets as she walked, her keys nudging against her fingers, ready to be grabbed and utilised as soon as she reached her vehicle, minimising the amount of time she'd be out in the freezing night.

The lighting in the car park wasn't as bright or plentiful as she'd like it to be, so it wasn't until she was twenty or so metres from her car that she realised someone was there, leaning against the bonnet. Someone much bigger than her, probably appearing larger still due to their own bulky outerwear.

She gasped, her pulse beginning to race, and stepped back, going instinctively for her keys as she did so. Unfortunately, she slipped on an icy manhole cover—the same one that almost got her the other day—and went over on the hard asphalt ground with a yelp, twisting her right ankle in the process. In amongst the shock and the pain flooding her system, she was vaguely aware of a man's voice.

"Shit! Oh my God, are you okay?" The man approached and loomed over her, a huge, shadowy figure. Terrified for her own safety, she tried to push herself away, but succeeded only in hurting herself more. She cried out in a mixture of agony and panic. Even without an injury, she'd have little chance of defending herself against this enormous bloke. Right now, she was completely screwed. She could scream, but who would hear? And even if they did, would they know where it had come from and arrive in time to help? "Rosie, stop. Stop, please. It's okay, it's okay. It's me, Luke."

His words finally penetrated through the fog of fear and pain, and she stopped trying to get away. She was safe. She was hurting, a lot, but she was safe. Luke would never hurt her—or anyone else for that matter. Wincing, she looked up at him in the dim light and squeaked out a "Hi."

He gave a wry smile. "Hi. Come on, let me help you up."

For some reason, his words came across as an order rather than an offer of assistance and instantly got her back up. She ignored his outstretched hand, took a deep breath and tried to swallow the pain. "I can manage, thank you."

Luke held his hands up in surrender and took a step back. "Okay, whatever you say." While his tone had been casual, relaxed, his expression was full of concern.

Rosie dragged in another breath, pulled her feet beneath her, then attempted to stand. Unfortunately, while her left ankle did its job with only the mildest twinge of protest, trying to put weight on her right triggered what felt like every pain receptor in her body and turned their dials up to eleven. If it hadn't been for Luke darting over and scooping his arm around her waist, she'd have fallen again. She looked up at him through watery eyes. "Th-thanks."

"You're welcome. Have you got all your stuff?"

She squinted at the ground around them, then clumsily checked her pockets. Her bag was zipped up, so nothing could have escaped from there. It remained hooked over her shoulder. "Yes, looks like it."

"Great. Pop your arm around my neck, and we'll get you to your car. It's much too cold to start checking you over out here."

This time, she didn't resist—orders or not. Unfortunately, their height difference made that particular method of assisted travel almost impossible, and after spending almost a minute going barely anywhere, Luke let out a grunt of impatience. "You're not going to like this, but it'd be a lot easier and quicker if you'd let me carry you. *And* safer."

She'd been on the verge of protesting again until he'd added the last bit. He was right on all three counts, of course, but the final one really did make sense. If her injury—whatever that turned out to be—was exacerbated thanks to her stubbornness, or worse, if Luke himself got hurt, she'd have no one to blame but herself. And she was already beating herself up more than enough lately as it was. "Okay," she mumbled, as her right ankle began to throb, "but please be careful. This car park gets next to no sun, especially at this time of year, so it's a bit slippery."

To his credit, he made no comment about the fact *her* slipping over had caused this whole scenario in the first place. "I will, I promise. Okay, just stand there a moment." He disentangled from their current hold, then eased her into his arms. Slowly, but not as slowly as when she'd been attempting to hop, Luke made his way to her car. Once he was at the passenger side, he slowly lowered her to the ground.

"What are you doing?" she asked, gasping at the cold of the metal against her palm as she braced it on the vehicle.

"Driving you home, of course. You can't drive with one foot. It's not safe *or* legal. Then we can see what the damage is." He held out his hand. "Keys, please."

She shot him a look of disgust, but retrieved the keys from her coat pocket and passed them to him. He pressed the button to unlock the car, then opened the passenger side door and helped her in. Once he was sure she'd got both legs safely inside, he closed the door, went around to the driver's side, and climbed in.

Despite her extreme discomfort, Rosie couldn't help sniggering as Luke sat crammed into her car, his knees practically up to his chin. "Seat adjuster's underneath, in the middle," she supplied, after watching him awkwardly grope around for a few seconds.

"Thanks." There came a ratcheting sound, followed by a *clunk*, and suddenly Luke was in a much more comfortable-looking driving position. The top of his head was brushing the ceiling, but there was no point making that seat adjustment for such a short journey. He could manage. "There." He glanced over. "Have you got your belt on?"

She pulled the seatbelt from its housing and clicked it into place, while Luke did the same. Then he inserted the key into the ignition, checked the vehicle wasn't in gear, and fired up the engine. He took a moment to locate the headlights, flipped them on, then slowly backed from the space, turned the car and drove it towards the car park exit. "So," he said, pulling up to the give way lines where the car park met the main road, "where am I going?"

"Oh." Rosie blinked and shook her head. She'd been so wrapped up in the embarrassment and pain of the situation she found herself in that she'd completely forgotten Luke had no idea where she lived. Which, she suspected, was the entire reason he'd been loitering by her car in the first place. But she certainly wasn't going to bring that up—not at the moment. "Sorry. Yeah. I'll direct you as we go. Left here."

They made the journey in silence, bar her directional

commands and the *click-click, click-click* of the indicators at the relevant times. Rosie tried to kid herself it was because Luke was concentrating on driving carefully in the dark, in a vehicle that wasn't his, to somewhere he wasn't familiar with, and with an injured passenger. Realistically, he probably wasn't speaking because he was pissed off with her for ignoring his messages and calls, which had now resulted in her with a knackered ankle and him playing chauffeur.

By the time she directed him onto her driveway, the pain had mutated from a sharp, bright pain to a burning throb. Hopefully that meant it was a sprain, rather than a break. She was still desperate to get some painkillers down her throat, though.

Still in silence, Luke parked the car, turned off the lights and engine, then pocketed the keys, got out, and made his way around to the passenger side. As he walked, she undid her seatbelt, and as soon as the door opened, she slowly rotated in her seat, grimacing when she caught her right foot on the doorjamb, sending a spear of pain lancing through her ankle. Tears welled in her eyes. "Fuck, that hurt."

"Come on," Luke said softly, "let's get you inside and check things out." He helped her from the seat, lifted her into his arms, then used his hip to bump the car door closed. "Can you reach into my right coat pocket for the keys?"

Rosie found them, and pushed the button to lock the vehicle. The reassuring *thunk* sounded as Luke strode towards the front door. Once there, bathed in the glow from the motion-activated security light, he took in the beautiful Christmas wreath hanging there and said, "Er, house keys?"

Her front door key was on the bunch she still held, so she encouraged him to move a little closer, so she could reach to slide it into the lock and turn it. She depressed the handle and pushed the door open, then said, "Head in, make a right and go one pace, so I can turn the alarm off before it starts screeching, please."

The alarm safely deactivated, they muddled through closing and locking the front door and switching on some lights before Luke asked, "Where's the sofa?"

"Just through there." She pointed.

Luke carried her through, and Rosie slapped another light switch on the way past. Her lovely, cosy living room came into view, still bearing all its Christmas finery, and suddenly she realised how weird it felt for Luke to be there. In her safe space. The very place where she'd spent the last few evenings angsting over whether they had a future or not.

Still, she could hardly kick him out. Well, she could, but even stubborn as she was, she recognised the next little while would be a damn sight easier with someone around to help. Calling her parents was an option, of course, but she didn't want them to have to come out in the cold and the dark, especially since they were still recovering from the nasty virus. Plus, Luke was *right here.* Sending him away would be idiotic.

He deposited her gently onto the sofa, then straightened. "Right, shall I get the heating on? Where's your thermostat?"

She shook her head. "It should already have kicked in. I turned it on from my phone before I left the shop."

He moved over and pressed his hand to the nearest radiator, then snatched it back with a hiss. "Oh yeah, that's on. Brilliant. Gotta love technology. Here, let me take your coat, hat and scarf."

Rosie deposited her bag on the floor by her feet, then took off her hat and scarf and handed them to Luke. He placed them on an end table before removing his own and dropping them on top of hers, then turned back to her.

Ditching her coat was considerably more difficult, since she was reluctant to put any weight on her injured ankle and didn't want to attempt it on one leg. Instead, she stayed sitting and made a ridiculous song and dance of it with lots of shuffling and leaning from side to side as she yanked at the garment. Eventually, she held it out to Luke, who wore the slightest smirk. "I'll hang this up in the hall." He took it from her, scooped the hats and scarves from the end table, and disappeared into the hallway.

A moment later he came back, *sans* coat and boots. "Sorry for coming in with my boots on, but they were extenuating circumstances." He gave a tight-lipped smile. "Now, shall we see about yours?" He crouched in front of her, empathy written all over his face. "The bad one's the right one, yeah?"

She nodded and bit her lip, not at all looking forward to what would happen next.

"Okay. Let's start with the easy bit." He unzipped her left boot, removed it from her foot and placed it on the carpet. "There. Now let's see what the damage is. Brace yourself. I'll be as gentle as I can."

He was gentle, too, holding the sole of her boot while

creeping the zip down, so there was minimal pulling against her ankle. When it was fully undone, he began to ease the boot off, glancing up at her face periodically to make sure she was okay. He managed to get it off with Rosie only snatching in one pained breath through her clenched teeth—not a bad result, all things considered. He discarded the footwear, then looked up at her, his lips pressed into a flat line. "Socks now, I think. I'll have to do both, so I can see the difference between the injured one and the uninjured one."

"That makes sense," Rosie said, then cringed. "I apologise in advance for the stinky feet."

Luke rolled his eyes good-naturedly. "Least of my worries right now, sweetheart. You ready?"

She nodded. "Left first."

"Left first," he agreed. Thankfully, her socks were made of quite stretchy material, and he took the first off with no trouble at all. He tossed it towards her boots. "Okay. Now for the other one. Ready?"

"As I'll ever be." If she weren't in so much pain, she'd probably be dying of embarrassment right now. First her ex-boyfriend had seen her go arse over tit in a car park, and now he was getting a nose full of her feet, which had been crammed into thick socks and heavy winter boots all day while she worked. Poor bloke was probably on the verge of passing out. But he seemed to be taking it in his stride, bless him.

As carefully as if he were handling a newborn baby, Luke rolled the sock from her bad foot. She clenched her jaw as he did so, pre-empting any stabs of agony. Thankfully, there weren't any—just continued throbbing, which was actually beginning to make her feel nauseous.

The second sock joined the first, and Luke cupped each of her calves and held her legs so her feet were side by side. He sucked in a breath through his nostrils and said gravely, "Yeah, some pretty bad swelling there. Is it okay if I check you over?"

"Yes. Thanks."

He inclined his head. "Sorry in advance if I hurt you." He asked a series of questions while looking over and lightly touching and manipulating her injured ankle. Finally, he said, "Obviously I'm no doctor, but as you know, I played a hell of a lot of football when I was younger, and I'm leaning towards a sprain, rather than a break. You didn't hear a crack or a pop when you went down, did you?"

"Only from the demolition of my dignity," she said wryly.

He chuckled. "Glad to see your sense of humour has remained intact. Seriously, though, what do you want to do? I'm happy to run you over to A&E if you'd like to get checked out by someone who actually knows what they're talking about. I can grab you some slip-on shoes if you tell me where to find them."

"No way." She shook her head emphatically. "A&E on a Saturday evening? Are you kidding? It'll be full of people with sports injuries, and the longer we're there we'll start getting the alcohol-related incidents coming in. No, it'll be carnage. I'll see how I go tonight. If I decide I want to go in the morning, I'll ring Dad and ask him to take me."

"As long as you're sure," he replied, narrowing his eyes at her. "It's honestly no trouble."

"I'm sure. Anyway, don't you have to be at work?"

"Nope, not tonight. So I'm afraid you're stuck with me. For a while, at least." He got to his feet, then grabbed a couple of cushions and piled them at the end of the sofa. "Right, get your foot up on there. I'm going to put the kettle on and find you an ice pack and some ibuprofen."

He strode off, as luck would have it, in the direction of the kitchen, leaving Rosie gaping at his rapidly-retreating back.

She groaned as she swung her legs up onto the sofa. So much for her quiet, relaxing evening.

Chapter Sixteen

Luke returned from the kitchen within a few minutes, a glass of water in one hand and a small red box in the other. A pack of frozen peas and a tea towel were trapped between his elbow and his side. He dropped them onto the sofa near her feet. "Here you go," he said, handing her the glass, then opening the box, removing the blister pack, and popping two ibuprofen into his palm, which he held out.

"Thanks," she said, then took the tablets and tipped them into her mouth, before chasing them down with water. She swallowed hard, then downed the rest of the water and passed the glass back to Luke.

"Good girl." He nodded approvingly, then scooped up the tea towel, placed it over the bare skin of her ankle, then carefully laid the bag of frozen peas on top. Almost immediately, the cooling effect sent relief coursing through her. "There. You arrange that how you want it. I'll be right back with your tea. Sit tight." He headed for the kitchen once more.

Rosie tweaked the position of the ice pack, then grabbed two more cushions and stuffed them behind her, before sinking into them with a sigh. Her ankle felt a smidge better now it was being iced, but she had no doubt it was a temporary fix, and hoped the painkillers would kick in quickly, dialling down both the pain and the swelling. She mentally crossed her fingers it was only a sprain. That was bad enough, but a break would be way worse. Either way, it was a huge inconvenience.

She closed her eyes and let her head loll back, wallowing in self-pity. Hot tears seeped from the outer corners of her eyes and ran into her hairline. God, she was *such* an idiot! She'd been so set on ignoring Luke in order to protect her emotions that she'd not only ended up hurting herself physically, but now she was pretty much dependent on him to help her—a kind of psychological torture. Served her right, really. As Ingrid had pointed out, her behaviour had to be hurting Luke, so if this was her punishment, she had no right to complain.

The click of ceramic on coaster reached her ears, and she opened her eyes to see Luke straightening from where he'd placed a cup of tea on the end table nearest her head. "Thanks."

"You're welcome." He lowered himself into an armchair, holding another cup of tea.

"Oh," she gave him a pointed look, "made yourself one too, did you?"

"Yes, I bloody well did." He cupped the mug in his large hands, steam wafting towards his face. "It's freezing outside, and I'd been standing there ages waiting for you. I wasn't sure if the shop closed at five or half past, and I didn't want to risk missing you."

Rosie's eyebrows leapt up almost of their own accord. "I didn't ask you to wait for me in the freezing cold."

"Maybe not, but you didn't exactly give me much other choice, did you?"

A sinking feeling took over her. She'd known the topic would have to come up, but she'd hoped to put it off a while longer. "W-what do you mean?"

Luke gave her a level stare. "You know perfectly well what I'm talking about, Rosie. You've been ignoring me since Boxing Day. And I'd like to know why. I went off to work, happy as Larry, thinking we might be starting something again, then... nothing. At first I thought perhaps you were tired, busy, distracted. But then it became blindingly obvious you were deliberately not answering me." He sighed. "I didn't know where you lived, only where you worked, and I didn't think you'd appreciate me showing up at the shop while you had customers and staff in, so my best option was to wait by your car so I could speak to you by yourself. And look how that's ended up."

"Well, I suppose you're glad I've been punished for ignoring you," she said archly.

"Don't be ridiculous," he snapped, his eyes flashing with anger. "I'm at least partly responsible for what happened, and I feel dreadful about it. You know damn well *that*," he jerked his chin at her elevated foot, "isn't the kind of pain I'm into." Luke sat back heavily in his chair, narrowly avoiding spilling tea over himself in the process.

Silence hung in the air, so thick Rosie fancied she could reach out and touch it. Instead, she stared sullenly at the packet of peas covering her swollen ankle, part of her wanting to tell Luke to get out, while at the same time recognising if she did, she would be forced to either struggle through the rest of the evening and night alone, or phone her parents. Neither of those options was preferable, so she kept her mouth shut.

From the corner of her eye, she saw Luke take a sip of his

tea, then lean forward to place the mug on a coaster on her coffee table. "So," he said quietly, "are you going to tell me what's going on? Or do I have to drag it out of you?"

Bloody hell, he sounds like Ingrid. The in-pain, grumpy side of her wanted to respond with his second option, but she took a deep breath and engaged her rational side. She'd treated him badly enough, without her taking her irritability out on him, too— particularly when he'd looked after her so well. "I'm..." She stared at him. Stared at the beautiful, sexy, smart, caring man who'd commandeered a good chunk of her adult romantic life, even when he'd been living on the other side of the Atlantic Ocean, completely unaware of her continued feelings for him. Wondered at how he remained so calm on the surface, when he had to be fuming with her. And rightly so.

But then, control was his thing. Both inside and outside the bedroom, he was incredible at keeping his cool, which made him an amazing Dom, as well as a brilliant chef and all-round human being. It was also why, when people *did* see glimpses of irritation or anger from him, they knew they'd really touched a nerve.

She huffed out a breath through her nostrils. If he was that perfect, why was she resisting so damn hard? She still loved him, he still loved her... what the hell was her problem? Hadn't enough time been wasted already?

She tried again. "I'm... fucked up. That's what's going on."

Luke raised one eyebrow, then retrieved his mug and took a sip of tea, watching her the entire time over the rim, his dark eyes assessing. "O...kay," he finally replied, placing his drink back on its coaster, "could you elaborate, please, and also explain how it relates back to us?"

Rosie clenched her jaw so hard she feared she'd crack some teeth. He was being *too* damn calm, and all it was doing was winding her up. He might have as much crap whirling around his brain as she did, maybe more, but with that inscrutable expression on his stupidly handsome face, he gave off the air of a man who didn't have a single care in the world. How bloody infuriating.

She had cares, though, lots of them. And she couldn't keep them in a second longer. "I'm just so fucking pissed off, all right? It took me a hell of a long time to get over losing you—though if I'm being honest, I don't think I ever *did* fully get over it. Anyway, I'm at a good place in my life now—my own business, my own house, car, friends, whatnot—and then *you* show up and turn everything upside down. As if that weren't bad enough, you then tell me you were going to bloody well *propose* to me that night we split up. I mean, what the fuck? I could have had an incredible wedding to a man I was madly in love with and an insane adventure in New York City. And what did I get instead? To stay exactly where I was, doing exactly what I was doing, only to jack it all in eventually anyway. I made a decision, the *wrong* decision, and I've had to live with it."

Luke frowned. "But you said it yourself, you're in a good place in your life right now. You love what you're doing. That might not have happened if things hadn't worked out the way they did. I'm not saying I was ever *happy* about it, far from it, but I did come to terms with it—eventually."

"But we could have been *married,* Luke. Could have had

kids. Me being a fucking wimpy idiot stopped that from coming to pass."

"You're talking as though this is an either/or situation. It totally isn't. If it's what you want, we could still get married, still have kids. Granted, I'm not getting any younger, but hopefully there's time yet. I mean, if De Niro can do it at seventy-nine, I should be okay at forty-two."

"But we could have had *more* time. Ten fucking years, to be exact!" The hot tears sprung up again, this time spilling down her cheeks in what felt like an endless stream. "We've wasted so much time. Well, I have. I've deprived us both of a whole decade of life together. Married life. Life as parents. Happiness." She squeezed her eyes closed as another thought occurred to her. "I even deprived your *mum* of the chance to be a grandmother. Your poor mum. Th-there's no fixing that, is there?" She opened her eyes again and looked at him, though through the tears he was a complete blur. Maybe it was just as well. She didn't really want to see his reaction to the thought of what his mother had missed out on. "How can you ever forgive me for being such a spineless arsehole?"

A large, fuzzy shape filled her vision. She blinked, revealing Luke gingerly lowering himself onto the very edge of the sofa, careful not to jostle her. He grabbed her hands and peered earnestly into her face. "Rosie, I told you before, there's nothing to forgive. Not a damn thing. You didn't do anything wrong. At the time it wasn't what you wanted, and that's completely fine. I refuse to worry about the intervening years, or think about how things might have been different. There's no point. We can't change the past, so why torture ourselves over it?"

He paused, squeezed her hands. "All I'm interested in is the here and now—and the future. Losing Mum has really driven that home for me. Yes, she'd have adored being a grandma, would have spoiled any children we had rotten. But just because that can't happen now doesn't mean we shouldn't give things another shot. All that's doing is punishing ourselves for things outside our control. We shouldn't deprive ourselves of the beautiful wedding, the opportunity to be parents, deprive my dad and your parents of the chance to be grandparents. James of the chance to be an uncle. I think…" he pulled their joined hands to his chest, and fixed her with a meaningful look, "what actually needs to happen is for you to forgive yourself. Let go of whatever's holding you back, and let's move forward together. You love me, don't you?" There was no mistaking the doubt in his voice at the last question.

She sniffed and nodded, her heart pounding and head whirling. "Yes, but… what if it doesn't work out between us? I-I told you, I don't think I can put myself through that again."

Finally, Mr Cool as a Cucumber started to lose it. He sighed heavily, his shoulders slumping. Weariness edged his tone as he said, "Rosie, you can't live your life based on what-ifs. It's no life at all. You don't stop yourself getting into a car just in case you have a crash, do you? Don't avoid crossing roads in case you're run over? There are absolutely no guarantees in life, not of safety, not of happiness, not of health. Look at Mum. Here one minute, gone the next. But at least when she *did* go, she had the two people she loved most by her side. I don't know about you, but when I'm on my deathbed, I don't want to have regrets hanging over me. And if I don't throw everything I've got at persuading you to give us another shot, I *will* regret that."

He lowered their hands to his lap and gazed at them for a moment, then looked up at her, his eyes wet. "Rosie, I can't guarantee every aspect of our life will be perfect. I can't guarantee our wedding will go without a hitch. I can't guarantee our flight won't be delayed when we go on our honeymoon. I can't guarantee you'll get pregnant precisely when we'd like you to. I can't guarantee you'll sail through your pregnancy or pregnancies with no issues. I can't guarantee our babies will be little angels who sleep eight hours a night, every night from the moment we bring them home. What I *can* guarantee is that I will be there, by your side, every step of the way, as much as it's in my power to do so. I *can* guarantee I will love you, do everything I can to make you happy, support you, be your partner in every way and give you what you need. So, what do you say? We can take things as slow, or as fast, as you like." His eyes filled with hope and one corner of his lips quirked up. "Come on, Kilbride. Shall we give this another shot?"

Chapter Seventeen

Rosie stared at Luke in silence, her brain whipped up in a tornado of thoughts, questions, and emotions. Her blood thundered in her ears, making it even harder to concentrate on what was happening. She took a deep breath and forced herself to focus. Despite her screwing it all up ten years ago, he was here, offering her a second chance. He was willing to put the past behind them and move on. He didn't even blame her for what happened.

If Luke was eager to try again, why wasn't she?

The answer was blindingly obvious. It was the same damn reason it had been a decade ago. Because she was too fucking scared. Too terrified of the unknown to take a leap.

She eased her hands from his and clenched them into fists.

No. I'm not having that. I'm not the same woman I was back then. I've grown, changed. Matured. Taken leaps. And besides, this isn't the unknown. It's Luke. I just need to be—

"Brave," she said out loud. "I wasn't brave enough back then. But I am now. I was stupid to throw away what we had, but I won't be that stupid again."

He regarded her quizzically, hopefully. "Is that a—"

"Yes. It's a yes!" She threw her arms around his neck, the movement sending a sharp stab of pain through her ankle. She gasped and held onto him, tears springing to her eyes. But they weren't just tears of pain. They were tears of relief, of happiness. Once the wave of agony had passed, leaving more nausea in its wake, she murmured into his ear, "I'm so, so sorry for ignoring you these last few days. It was wrong, and a really horrible thing to do. I feel terrible about it. I just… didn't know what to do." She sniffed, hugged him tighter. "I don't deserve you. I-I told you I was fucked up."

Luke shifted his arms from where they'd been wrapped around her back, clapped his hands onto her shoulders and eased her away from him. When his face came into focus, his expression was stern. "Listen to me, Rosie. I don't want any more of this self-flagellation from you, all right? And this is the last time I'm going to say it: ten years ago, you did nothing wrong, so there was nothing for me to forgive you for. This week… well, yes," he nodded, "admittedly you've been a bit of an arsehole and seriously put me through the wringer. But you've apologised, you've explained why, and I understand. I forgive you, and I'd very much like to move on, okay?"

He cupped her face, used his thumbs to gently wipe away her tears, then dropped a soft, toe-curling kiss to her lips. This time when he came back into focus, he was smirking. "Besides, if anyone's going to flagellate you, it's going to be me."

Rosie couldn't help the snort which escaped her. *Trust him to make a smutty joke at a time like this.* She aimed a playful whack at his arm. "Perv!"

"That's me." He gave her another quick kiss, which, despite the brevity, still made her stomach flip, then dropped his hands from her face and got up. "Now," he said as he crossed back to the armchair and sat in it, "drink your tea before it gets cold, then we'll figure out some food. You shouldn't really have had those ibuprofen on an empty stomach, but needs must."

Food. Oh, fuck! Rosie let out a groan as she picked up her cup of tea. *This is turning out to be one hell of a day.*

"Hey, are you all right? I could have passed that to you if you were struggling that much. You're not hurt anywhere else, are you?"

She shook her head, even as she wanted to melt at the level of his concern. "I'm all right, honest. I just remembered I wasn't coming straight home from work. I was going via the supermarket. To get something in for my dinner tonight, as well as for tomorrow. Me, Mum and Dad are having our Christmas Day re-do." She glanced disdainfully at her ankle. "Or we *were,* anyway. Fuck's sake! I'm going to have to cancel."

"No you're not."

She wrinkled her nose at him. "What are you talking about? How the hell am I supposed to cook a Christmas roast on one bloody leg? I'm not a sodding flamingo."

"You're not," he said matter of factly, then sipped his tea. "I am."

Rosie shook her head, then smiled wryly. "That's lovely of you, but you can't cook fresh air. Even *you're* not that good a chef."

"Thank you, I *think,*" he drew his eyebrows together thoughtfully, "for that backhanded compliment. But you're making this way more complicated than it needs to be. I'll finish my tea, then head to the supermarket. As long as you don't mind me driving your car without you in it. If so, I can always call an Uber. I take it you've got a list?"

"Yes, but—"

"But nothing. Have you already forgotten what I said? About supporting you? Or in this case, helping you? I know this whole thing has been a bit of a whirlwind—trust me, I know—so it'll take time to settle into whatever our relationship is going to look like, but me popping to the shop on your behalf really isn't a big deal. I'd do it for anyone I cared about. I don't have work tonight, don't have any plans. I can do the shopping, make you some dinner, help you get ready for bed, then head home. I'll come back in the morning and crack on with the roast."

"Don't you have work tomorrow?"

"Yes, but not until the evening." He downed his tea, then returned the cup to its coaster. "So, what's it to be? Do I need to order an Uber?"

Rosie blinked. It looked like the plan was decided. "No, of course not. You can take my car. I think I put the keys in my coat pocket." She put her drink down, then snagged the handle of her handbag and swung it onto her lap. "Let me find the list, and my credit card."

"Just the list is fine. I don't want to get done for fraud if someone catches me using your card." He stood and crossed over to her, then held his hand out for the list. "I'll stick it on mine, then you can bank transfer the amount to me later." He took the notepad from her, then examined the top page's contents. After a moment, he nodded. "Okey dokey." He leaned down and kissed her. It was more than a peck, but less than a lingering snog, and latent with enough promise that it made her heart race. When he pulled away, he was grinning from ear to ear. "Do you need anything before I go?

Another drink? Help to the loo?"

She shook her head. "I'm good, thanks. I have a downstairs toilet—if I need to go while you're gone, I can hop there and back."

He sobered. "Well, be careful, won't you? I don't want to come back to more injuries."

"I'll be careful."

"Good girl." He dropped another kiss on the top of her head, then stepped towards the hallway.

Before he could get too far, she said, "Oh. You know the lasagne on the list?"

He paused, one eyebrow lifted in query. "What about it?"

"Make sure it's big enough for two people." She looked him in the eye and smiled, hoping her meaning was clear.

Luke returned her smile. He got it. "Will do." He carried on walking.

"And Luke?"

He stopped again, now with one foot out the door. "Yes?"

"Could you also get some—"

"Garlic bread?" he finished with a smirk.

She nodded, her smile widening. "Yes, please. See you later. Don't be long."

"I will be as quick as safely and humanly possible. Just you rest that foot, all right?" He disappeared into the hallway, and she heard him shuffling around, presumably putting on his shoes, coat, hat and scarf. Finally, there came the jingle of keys, and a "See you later. Love you!"

Her responding "Love you, too" was lost in the closing of the front door. She watched him pass by the front window towards the car, heard him open and close the door, then fire the engine. The headlights flicked on, making her close her eyes to avoid the harsh light as he reversed off the drive, since the beams landed directly on the window. When she cracked them open seconds later, he was gone.

In the silence left behind, Rosie scooped up her cup of tea and stared into space as she drank it, feeling steamrollered by the day. The shocker she'd had in the shop and the incident in the car park had been bookended by bollockings from Ingrid *and* Luke—albeit ones she both deserved and needed to hear—and she was really only just getting the opportunity to catch up. To process what the hell had gone on, and what it meant.

Who was she kidding? She knew *exactly* what it meant. Sod all the ins and outs, the whats and the whys—she and Luke were back together. Something she'd wanted for a very long time, but had fully believed could and would never happen. Not in a million years.

It hadn't worked for them before, but that didn't mean it wouldn't work now. Things were different. Besides, so many things had had to fall into place in a precise way to ensure they were in the same place at the same time on Christmas Day. Maybe the universe really had brought them back together for a reason.

Against so many odds, her ghost of Christmas past had become her ghost of Christmas present.

She still wasn't sure of much else, but she was sure she *really* wanted him to be her ghost of Christmas future, too. Well, less a ghost, and more a living, breathing man.

Luke's sudden arrival in her life had convinced her she'd been on Santa's naughty list this year. But actually, once she cast aside her regrets and fears, she realised she'd had it arse-backwards.

She grinned widely as joy, anticipation and excitement filled her being. Never mind his good list—clearly, she'd been on Santa's best-girl-ever list.

Chapter Eighteen

Rosie lowered her fork to her empty plate, then sat back in her chair at the kitchen table with a satisfied groan. They'd positioned themselves so Rosie could rest her right foot on a cushion on the seat of the chair to her right, and Luke sat to her left, keeping his long legs well out of her way. She rubbed her tummy. "God, that was good."

Luke shot her an amused glance as he chewed his last chunk of garlic bread. He swallowed, then said, "I wish I could take the credit, but all I did was pull stuff out of packets and put them on baking trays, then in the oven. Hardly cooking, is it?" He shuddered. "But you're right, it *was* good. Not as good as my homemade lasagna, obviously, but delicious nonetheless. And it filled a hole."

She snickered. "Modest as ever, I see."

"Naturally." He wiggled his eyebrows. "So, what are we having for dessert?"

Rosie's mouth dropped open. *Shit!* While she'd had the foresight to amend her supermarket order to get a bigger lasagna as well as the garlic bread, since she had a guest, she hadn't considered a dessert. She didn't generally bother when she was by herself—finding it easier to grab a couple of biscuits or a snack-sized chocolate bar to appease her craving for something sweet—maybe ice cream in the warmer months. And at this time of year, there was always plenty of chocolate and sweets in the house. "I, er, don't have anything, I'm afraid. I didn't think—"

The huge grin taking over Luke's face stopped her in her

tracks. "I'm winding you up. I just wanted to see your reaction." He chuckled. "I'm more than happy to help you make a dent in the dozens of boxes of goodies piled up on the sideboard. I hate to think of you wading through them all by yourself."

"Oh, that's *so* generous of you," she quipped, then stuck her tongue out at him. "I bought a couple of the boxes, but the majority were gifts. From friends, but mostly from clients and customers of the shop. You should see *inside* the sideboard. I've got umpteen bottles of wine, gin, cream liqueur and sherry in there. I'm hoping to foist the sherry off on Mum tomorrow. I—"

"Can't stand the stuff," he put in, nodding. "I remember." He paused, licked his lips, then fixed her with a serious gaze. "I remember everything about you, Rosie. I know it's mushy as fuck, but even though we've been thousands of miles apart for years, you've always been in here," he tapped his chest, then his head, "and here. In truth, as much as I barely admitted it, even to myself, I always harboured a hope we'd get a second chance one day." He reached across the table and took her hand, his touch warm, comforting. Loving. "It's the best Christmas present I could have ever wished for."

Her heart fluttered as they stared into each other's eyes. She swallowed hard, tears welling up. "It's the best Christmas present I could have ever wished for, too."

Luke smiled, then lifted her hand to his lips and pressed a kiss to her knuckles, the brush of his beard against her skin sending a shiver of delight through her. "Glad to hear it." He released her, then pushed his chair back. "Right, I'm going to get cleared up."

Before she could protest—not that her bad ankle would make it easy for her to do the job herself—he was on his feet and gathering up their plates.

She watched silently, helplessly, as Luke glided around her kitchen, collected everything that needed to be collected and popped it into the dishwasher, sprayed and wiped the worksurfaces and the table, then turned to her with the empty food packaging in hand. "Where's your outside bin? You don't want this stinking up the place, do you?"

She screwed up her nose and shook her head. "It's out the back. Just through that door there. Turn right and you'll see it. Key's on the hook hidden behind that peace lily."

Luke gave a nod of understanding, then, to her amusement and surprise, crammed his feet into the purple rubber slip-ons she kept by the door and shuffled off to complete his self-appointed task, his heels hanging off the back of the too-small footwear. After it closed behind him, she stared at the door he'd just exited, trepidation skittering through her and obliterating her mirth at the shoe situation as she wondered what was going to happen next. It was eight-thirty—already way past the time she'd usually be in her pyjamas when spending an evening in on her own. A shower was out of the question, but she could run a bath—just to clean herself, rather than to have her usual luxurious soak, and hopefully Luke would help her get into it. She groaned at the indignity of it—but what choice did she have? She could strip wash at the sink, she supposed, but it'd be much harder work to stand on one leg *and* get clean than it would to simply sit in the bath. Once she was in the tub, she'd be fine. And maybe some heat on her ankle would be nice, too. If not, she'd have to hang it over the side.

A whoosh of cold air hit her as Luke burst back inside, his shoulders hunched up to his ears and the part of his cheeks visible over his beard flushed pink. He kicked off her shoes, then closed and locked the door and returned the key to its spot, before turning to her, rubbing his hands together. "Phew—it's bloody freezing out there!"

She smiled. "Thank you for doing that. And for, well," she wafted her hand around vaguely, "everything you've done. I appreciate it."

Luke moved over to the kitchen radiator and stood with his back to it, his hands flattened against its surface. He flashed her a mischievous grin. "Does that include me persuading you to give us another go?"

"Too soon to say," she shot back, mirroring his grin. "You never know—it could be the biggest mistake we've ever made. We might get fed up of each other."

"We miiight," he said with a shrug. "Or we might end up even crazier about each other than we were before."

She smirked, suspecting he was probably correct, but having no intention of telling him so. "I guess only time will tell." She paused and screwed up her lips before continuing with, "Speaking of time… it's getting late. Do you think you could help me upstairs and into the bath, please? I figure it's the easiest and safest way for me to wash. My hair can wait another day or so. I can dig out some dry shampoo."

Luke nodded. "'Course." He looked around, his glance stopping on the back door and the oven. "Everything's sorted and safe down here, so do you want to head up now?"

"Please. If it's not too much trouble."

He stepped away from the radiator and crossed the room towards her. "When it comes to you, nothing is too much trouble."

"Oh, you sweet talker, you."

"That's me. Right, let's pull your chair out… that's it… hold on to me… and… there we go!" He hoisted her into his arms and made his way from the kitchen to the living room, then out to the hall, careful not to bash Rosie on the doorframes. She hit light switches as they passed them, plunging most of the downstairs into darkness—barring the twinkling fairy lights on her Christmas tree and adorning her windowsills, some shelves and her mantlepiece. She'd asked Luke to turn them on when he got back from the supermarket, thinking they'd add a little cheer—plus she wanted to make the most of them, since she'd be taking them down before long. They were all on timers, so would automatically shut off after a couple more hours.

At the bottom of the stairs, she flicked on the light to illuminate the upstairs landing. "I can switch this one," she indicated the fixture above them, "off from up there."

"Good stuff." He stood at the bottom of the steps, peering up doubtfully.

She frowned. "What's the matter? Am I too heavy?"

He looked at her, amusement in his eyes. "Of course not. It's just quite a narrow staircase, and I'm trying to figure out how to get us up there safely *and* without bashing your ankle. I don't think it'd work to turn sideways, like I do through the doors." He screwed his face up for a moment, then his expression cleared and she practically saw the light bulb appear above his head. "Got it. Why don't I give you a piggyback? It means you'll be vertical rather than horizontal, so I'll be able to keep your feet well away from the walls and doorframes."

The analgesics, which had taken her pain from a ten down to somewhere in the region of a more manageable four were slowly starting to wear off, so as far as she was concerned, any plan that prevented her damaged ankle from being nudged or knocked was a good one. "Why not? It'll be a damn sight easier than hopping or crawling."

He snickered. "A bit less amusing, perhaps."

She rolled her eyes as he lowered her to the carpet. "Sorry to have ruined your fun."

"Ahh, quit your whinging and get that gorgeous arse of yours on the fourth step."

Rosie did as he said, then waited until he turned his back on her before reaching out with both hands, grabbing handfuls of his demin-clad backside and giving a hearty squeeze. "I think you'll find *you're* the one with the gorgeous arse."

Luke whirled around, wagging his finger playfully. "Any more of that horseplay, young lady, and I'll have you over my knee."

Amusement tugged at the corners of her lips. "Is that supposed to put me off? Because that sounds like fun to me."

He groaned and slapped his hand to his head. "Damn it. What

have I done? I've created a monster."

"You didn't create her," she quipped, "you just enticed her out of her lair."

Their gazes clashed, and they dissolved into laughter—the resultant endorphins flooding Rosie's system keeping a lid on her physical discomfort, for now at least. The fact she and Luke were laughing and joking, flirting, exchanging banter as though the last ten years had never happened filled her full of euphoria. Maybe things really *could* work this time around. Maybe she should just let go of the past, of the doubts, the worries, and embrace the present. Let the future take care of itself.

When they finally calmed down, she climbed onto Luke's back and he carried her upstairs. "Where am I going?" he asked.

"Second door on the left," she replied, directing him straight to the bathroom, since all the giggling had suddenly made her *very* aware of the fullness of her bladder. "Could you put me down next to the loo, please, then give me some privacy? I'll shout you when I'm done."

"Sure."

Her toilet break took longer than planned due to her partial incapacity, but she called for Luke while she was drying her hands and he appeared in an instant. "Bloody hell, that was quick."

"I was right outside the door."

She pulled a face as she replaced the hand towel on its rail. "Eww. You listened to me peeing?"

"I didn't *listen*," he said with a tut. "I could *hear,* yes, but I didn't *listen.* I didn't dare go far in case you needed me."

"Aww," she said, softening. "That's so sweet. So…" she shifted her gaze to the tub, then back to his face, "ready to help me get naked, wet and soapy?"

Interest flared in his eyes. "What sort of a stupid question is *that*?"

Chapter Nineteen

Rosie yawned as she clung onto Luke's arm while he helped her into her pyjama bottoms. "Oh God, sorry. How rude of me. It just slipped out."

He eased the soft cotton trousers emblazoned with cartoon dogs up her legs then let go of the waistband when it was settled into the right place. "That's okay. You had a busy day, then a stressful evening. Plus an injury. No wonder you're wiped out." After pulling back the duvet, he helped her sit on the mattress.

"Not all of my evening was stressful," she replied with a small smile, swinging her legs around and up onto the bed so her bad ankle was elevated. "It'd have been a hell of a lot worse without you here. And I've enjoyed spending time with you."

Despite their flirting beforehand, Rosie's bathtime had actually been chaste and functional. Luke had been the perfect gentleman as he'd helped her undress, run the bath, then aided her getting into it. He'd perched on the closed toilet seat as she cleaned up, and they'd fallen into more general chatter, filling each other in on some of the less important and life-changing things which had happened over the last decade.

Then he'd helped her from the bath, into a robe and finally into her bedroom—where he'd continued his impeccable behaviour as he'd waited for her to dry herself, then passed her the various toiletries and lotions and potions she liked to use on her face and body after a bath or shower. He'd even gently smoothed some of the ibuprofen gel he'd picked up from the supermarket onto her ankle before heading to the bathroom to wash his hands—saving her from having to get up again. He'd been kind, caring, and incredibly patient. And even though she hadn't thought it possible, she'd loved him more with every passing moment.

Luke grinned. "It was a pleasure to assist you, madame," he teased, then his expression turned earnest. "And I've enjoyed spending time with you, too. Now, is there anything else you need before I head off? I'll get your phone, a glass of water, and painkillers. Some biscuits so you can eat them first thing, before taking more tablets. I'll be back early to help you get up and then start the meal prep. Is there a spare key I can take so I can let myself in?"

"Wow," Rosie replied, impressed. "You've got it all covered. Except..."

His brow creased. "Except what? What did I miss?"

"Nothing," she shook her head, "but... is there really any point in you going home? Particularly since you're planning on coming back first thing in the morning."

"Probably not. If you're okay with me staying over, I'm happy to. Means I can keep an eye on you, make sure you're all right."

"Why wouldn't I be okay with it?"

He lifted and dropped one shoulder. "I don't want you to feel... like we've got to, you know, be intimate. Just because I'm here overnight."

A splutter of laughter escaped Rosie. "*Be intimate*? Why are you being so polite all of a sudden? It's not like we haven't had sex before. Very recently. And it was wild."

"I know." He tilted his head back to look at the ceiling and let out a groan. "Trust me, I know. It's imprinted on my memory. But the other day was different. That was a spur of the moment thing when everything was up in the air." He righted his head and focused on her. "Now we're actually back together, I don't want to fuck everything up by rushing things or making assumptions, okay?"

She held his gaze. "Luke. I am a grown woman. I don't feel I *have* to do anything. What if I simply *want* to? And besides," she sat back against her pillows, folded her arms and fixed him with a stern stare, "who says you're sleeping in here? I do have a spare room, you know."

Luke's eyes widened as he blushed. "So much for not making assumptions."

Relaxing her arms with a giggle, Rosie replied, "I'm *kidding*, you idiot. Not about having a spare room—though it's chock full of my crafting stuff—but about you sleeping in it. Of course I want you in here with me. We can cuddle, chat. If something else happens, it happens. If it doesn't, it doesn't. How does that sound?"

"Heavenly."

"Good. Now, send your dad a message to let him know you won't be home, so he doesn't worry. Then do what you've got to do and get your sexy arse back in here with me."

"Yes, ma'am." He gave a mock salute. "Dad'll be delighted to hear the news that we're back together." With a grin, he hurried off.

Within ten minutes the house was locked up tight, the

security alarm set, and both bedside tables held a glass of fresh water and a hot cup of decaffeinated tea. Rosie's also had the promised phone and painkillers. She took her last dose of the day as Luke stripped down to his boxers and slipped under the duvet beside her.

She swallowed hard, making sure the little white pills went where they were supposed to, then reached over to the bedside table and swapped the glass for the cup. When she relaxed back into her pillows again, Luke was right there beside her, mirroring her actions.

He held his mug of tea next to hers. "Cheers."

Rosie clinked her mug against his. "Tea in bed? I'll definitely 'cheers' that."

"You'll get another one in the morning—only that one will contain caffeine."

"Ooh," she gave a mock shiver, "I'm excited already. I feel like downing this so I can go to sleep, and my delicious cup of caffeinated tea will come sooner. On the other hand, just being here with you, now, is nice."

"Nice?" Luke scrunched up his nose.

She nudged him. "*Yes*. After the few days we've had, the turmoil, the emotional upheaval, isn't it nice to just sit here, warm, comfy and cosy, happy and content in each other's company?"

He sipped his tea, swallowed, then nodded and turned to her with a smile. "You're right—it *is* nice." He cupped her face tenderly, swept his thumb back and forth on her cheek, his eyes full of intensity. "I love you."

Tiny bubbles fizzed and popped in her stomach. "I love you too." She twisted her head and kissed his palm. He slipped his arm around her back and eased her towards him so she was tucked into his side.

They cuddled in silence, drinking their tea and exchanging the occasional soppy smile. Rosie allowed her thoughts to meander as they wanted, and found the state of affairs in her brain more settled than they had been since she'd first encountered Luke in Ingrid's café on Christmas Day. Perhaps she'd done as much work on processing subconsciously as she had consciously. Whatever had happened, she was glad of it, because now she was finally ready to draw a line under the past and move forward.

After a while, they finished their drinks, had a toilet break, then got back into bed. They met in the middle, facing each other and wearing goofy grins, like a couple of lovestruck teenagers. Somewhere along the way, the mushy domestic mood had dissipated, only to be replaced by something way more charged. Despite her earlier *laissez-faire* attitude to them having sex, now it was at the forefront of her mind and what she wanted more than anything.

And yet, alongside her growing arousal was a considerable measure of nerves. Stupid, really, since Luke had already seen her naked twice this week, *and* they'd slept together. But, like he'd pointed out, the other day in The Creative Collective had been a spur of the moment thing, with no time for nerves, and her nakedness today had been out of necessity, rather than anything remotely sexual.

Rosie reached out with a slightly unsteady hand and slotted her fingers into the hair at Luke's temple, then shuffled closer and kissed him. The warm, natural scent of him hit her nostrils, accompanied by that of his cologne and a hint of what was probably his shampoo or shower gel. The smells were familiar, sure, but that certainly didn't make them, or Luke, any less sexy.

He broke their kiss, only to murmur, "I thought you were tired." Amusement laced his tone.

She smirked. "Not *that* tired."

The heat from his body radiated clean through her pyjamas as she pressed up against him, their resumed kiss soft and tender, almost tentative. He cupped the back of her head, but didn't attempt to take things up a notch.

They continued exploring each other's mouths, slowly and thoroughly, as if for the first time.

Before long, Rosie was in danger of spontaneously combusting. Every part of her ached for Luke, for them to be together as one—a sort of consummation of their newly-rekindled relationship. She remembered how incredible it had been the other day, how she'd felt like she was exactly where she was supposed to be, and she yearned to experience that again. Only this time face to face, so they could look into each other's eyes as pleasure built, assaulted them, and they eventually climaxed.

She let out an abandoned groan and sucked Luke's bottom lip into her mouth—something she knew drove him crazy.

He growled, whipped his hand from her head to her backside and hauled her roughly up against him. His already-hard cock pressed into her thigh, and she hooked her leg over his hip and eased closer, rubbed her groin against him. The movement sent a twinge of discomfort through her ankle, but the combination of happy hormones and analgesics racing through her system allowed her to ignore it. She had way more important things to worry about right now.

Luke's beard prickled her face as their kiss grew deeper, more frantic. Their mouths clashed and fought; their tongues danced and darted. Rosie became dizzy with lust, so dizzy it was like she and Luke were caught up in an impenetrable fog—everything around them invisible, except for each other.

Suddenly, Luke scooped his arm beneath her, then rolled them so she was on top. She pushed herself up so she was astride him, careful to put her weight on her left knee, keeping her right foot so it was almost hovering over the mattress.

His pupils wide and his cheeks flushed, Luke reached up and deftly undid the buttons of her pyjama top, then eased the sides apart. He flashed her a wolfish grin before raking his gaze down her exposed body, her bare breasts, her tummy—at least until he reached the waistband of her bottoms, which prevented any further ogling. "Gorgeous," he murmured, shoving her top off her shoulders, before tugging it from her arms and launching it across the room. "Beautiful. Simply stunning."

She basked happily in his compliments, then moaned as he cupped her breasts, his hands warm and strong on the soft, plump globes of flesh. She rolled her hips in response, grinding onto his erection and making them both gasp.

"Fuck." She fought to maintain some semblance of control, focused on his face—that handsome, beloved face—then feasted on the sight of his broad shoulders, his strong arms, the thick smattering of hair that scattered across his pecs and down his abdomen, before disappearing into the top of his boxers. "Oh," she purred, gently scraping her nails down his front from collarbone to hipbone, before curling her fingers around the waistband of his undies, "*these* have got to go."

Luke smirked, and jerked his chin towards her pyjama bottoms. "Likewise." With that, he sat up, grabbed her, and skilfully flipped them so she was flat on her back. He pressed a kiss to her forehead before scooting down the mattress—careful to avoid her right ankle—and ditching his boxers. The moment he'd discarded them, he turned his attention to her, a dangerous twinkle in his eye which made Rosie's already wet pussy wetter still.

He crawled up her supine form and settled his legs between hers and his weight on his elbows either side of her arms. The sensation of his bare abdomen against hers was sublime, the heat between them scorching. When his face was level with hers, he took her mouth in a powerful kiss that managed to be needy and possessive all at once. She succumbed, wrapped her arms around him and gave as good as she got, then gasped breathlessly when he pulled away suddenly, only to treat her to another of those animalistic, predatory smiles.

Then he made his way down her body, kissing and caressing as he went. Gentle kisses and nibbles, the occasional suckle, the glide and squeeze of his work-roughened hands—all were amazing, throwing copious amounts of fuel onto her erotic fire. By the time he reached her trousers, her hands ached from gripping the sheet beneath her and her head whirled with thoughts of what he might do next.

She didn't have to wonder for long. He took the utmost care in removing the pyjama bottoms, particularly when he drew near her right ankle. He even dropped the most featherlight of kisses onto her swollen flesh, causing goosepimples to break out on her entire body. Then he settled his big hands on the insides of her calves and smoothed them up towards her groin, pushing her legs apart and making room for himself as he went. The movement was slow, but steady, and by the time she was spread before him, she was too turned on, too eager for him to touch her pussy, to even care what she looked like.

Luke let out a groan that seemed to come from deep inside his chest. "Christ, Rosie. I've missed this. Missed *you*."

Before she could even attempt to engage her brain enough to respond, he'd buried his head between her thighs and clamped his mouth to her vulva. All conscious, sensible thought was completely obliterated as he sucked and nibbled on her labia, sending white-hot fire zooming out from her core to scorch along every nerve ending. She gripped the sheets, hung on for the ride as Luke ate her pussy as, well, as a man who'd been wanting to do so for a decade and been denied the opportunity to do so would.

He'd truly forgotten nothing as he pulled out all the tricks he knew pushed her buttons. His skill, his enthusiasm, his stamina soon paid off as she felt that delicious pressure building within. The fire continued to burn, the epicentre right at the point where Luke's mouth and tongue teased, tormented and titillated her sensitive flesh.

She was on the precipice; teetering. When Luke closed his lips around her swollen clit and sucked, she tumbled from the edge with a screech. Ecstasy slammed into her, waves of bliss rippling through her core over and over as she bucked and thrashed, powerless against the force of her orgasm.

Finally, when her body relaxed and she came back to herself, she cracked open her eyes to see Luke watching her, his expression awestruck. A glance much further down his body revealed his cock was still raring to go.

She gave a lopsided, slightly dopey grin and held her arms open wide, silently encouraging him to come to her.

He was there in a beat, looming over her. His awestruck expression had morphed into one of intense need. "God, Rosie, if that was half as incredible for you experiencing it as it was for me just watching, then it was mind-blowing."

She wrapped her arms around him as she nodded and whispered, "It was. Now please, make love to me."

"There's nothing on this earth I'd like more." He leaned down and slanted his lips over hers, taking her mouth with a passion that made a trickle of juices seep from her pussy. And the additional lubrication hadn't come a moment too soon, as then Luke entered her in one long, slow thrust, causing her eyes to roll back in her head.

Their groans combined, deep and guttural, as her internal walls stretched to accommodate him, her wetness making it a delicious, slick glide that she never wanted to end. But of course it did, and as Luke bottomed out, he stared down at her face, his eyes burning with need and intensity, a question within them.

Rosie responded by hooking her left leg over his calves, drawing his upper body down against hers, and tilting her hips up—wordless but clear signals that she was ready. She closed her eyes and hung on to him, revelling in the sensation of his scorching skin against hers, the flex of his muscles, his laboured breathing as he began to move within her.

She moaned, rolling with him as best she could without putting any stress on her bad ankle. Fortunately, Luke had it all under control as he established a long, slow, grinding motion that set off sparks of pleasure deep within her core as well as stimulating her clit. It wasn't long before she was entirely lost to sensation; to thrusting, rolling, grinding, grasping—all mixed in with the purest of happiness.

A tear trickled from the corner of her eye as her emotions threatened to overwhelm her. Quite aside from the physical sensations, she was full of happiness, contentment, a sense of belonging, and love. Luke was, and always had been, her soulmate. And now he was back in her life, she had no intention of letting him go again, not ever. Not for anything.

Just then, he murmured into her ear, "God, you feel amazing. I… really want us to come together. Do you think we can?"

With a grin, she replied, "We can certainly try. Let me…" She pushed her hand between their bodies and pressed her index and middle fingers against the swollen nub at the apex of her vulva, then urged Luke to keep moving. His rolling and grinding motions transferred into her hand, allowing her to direct the stimulation to exactly where she needed it. The pleasure grew, bloomed, a heavy throbbing emanating through the entirety of her clit. Her core rippled, dragging a strangled gasp from Luke.

"F…uck. Ro, baby… I won't be… long."

"It's okay, baby," she whispered, stroking his hair with her free hand, then dropping a kiss to his head, "it's okay. Come for me. I'll be right there with you."

Luke's thrusts became shallower, faster, but he still made sure each movement butted up against her fingers, her clit, and after a handful more thrusts, Rosie was wound tight, ready to blow. Just a little…

"Uhhhh." Luke froze, the powerful twitch of his cock inside her utterly sublime. Then he came in a series of tiny, jerky movements, the shift and pressure of his pubic bone sending her off after him.

"Ahhh, fuck!"

They grunted, groaned, and spasmed together, basking in their mutual ecstasy before falling silent and still.

Eventually, an involuntary ripple of her internal muscles, a tiny aftershock, pushed his softening cock out of her. Luke stirred, then shifted to lean his forehead against hers and stared deep into her eyes. "I love you, Rosie Kilbride. So fucking much."

She grinned. "I love you too, Luke Adams. So fucking much."

He kissed her, then carefully rolled over to lie beside her, before pulling her into his arms once more. Still feeling boneless, blissfully wrung out, she snuggled into him and fell asleep moments later, a beatific smile on her face.

Chapter Twenty

Sunday lunchtime

At 1 p.m. on the dot, Rosie's doorbell rang, drowning out the muted tones of Bing Crosby, whose festive tune had just come up on the Christmas playlist Rosie had running via her phone and a Bluetooth speaker. After a beat, there came the sound of a key turning in a lock, a door opening, then an exaggeratedly loud, "Coo-ee, only uuuus!" from Rosie's mum.

Luke turned from the hob and looked at Rosie, a mixture of panic and amusement on his face, before shifting his attention back to the task at hand. Rosie rolled her eyes and bit her lip. She'd sent her mum a message earlier that morning to let her and Rosie's dad know a guest was joining them for dinner—though she hadn't said who it was, knowing perfectly well her mother would have then bombarded her with questions. She'd also said to just go ahead and let themselves in with their key when they arrived, since she'd be busy in the kitchen.

Fortunately, she'd worded her message well enough that her mum had accepted all of the information without question. Though those would come soon enough, when she spotted Luke *and* found out about Rosie's sprained ankle.

The latter was actually feeling a lot better, and, confident it was only a sprain, Rosie had decided against a visit to A&E. She'd made an appointment with her GP via the NHS phone app for the following week just to make sure everything was healing as it should, and had promised Luke she would take it easy in the meantime.

That meant accepting a great deal of help from him to get up and about, then washed and dressed, *and* taking a back seat when it came to preparing the meal. Though she hadn't been completely useless—he'd left her situated at the kitchen table, everything she needed to peel and slice the potatoes and vegetables within easy reach for an hour while he'd gone home to get showered and changed. That and setting the table—after he'd located all the necessary accoutrements and handed them to her. Still, she had little choice, and it was what couples did for each other, wasn't it?

Couples. Being in a couple with Luke again didn't feel entirely real. At the same time, her contentment and happiness were such she suspected it was written all over her face—she probably had that "glow" people always said pregnant women had. And who knew? Maybe she'd enjoy *that* glow sometime in the not-too-distant future, too.

"Hi Mum, Dad," she called back. "Come straight through to the kitchen when you're ready!"

"Will do," Victoria trilled. "Just taking our coats and shoes off, and getting our slippers on."

That gave her and Luke a minute or so before chaos was unleashed. "You ready for this?" she said more quietly, for his ears only.

He glanced over his shoulder and flashed her a tight, nervous smile. "As I'll ever be."

She returned his smile, then blew him a kiss, wishing she could go over and give him a hug and an *actual* kiss. "It'll be fine.

Don't worry. They loved you before. I can't see how things would be any different this time around."

"That was befo—" He stopped abruptly as Victoria and Stephen bustled into the room.

"Ooh," Stephen said, rubbing his hands together in delight, "something smells delicious."

But Victoria, who'd entered the kitchen ahead of her husband, had stopped dead and was staring open-mouthed at the tall, good-looking man currently commandeering her daughter's stove. Rosie's heart pounded as she stared at the bottle of red wine clutched in her mother's hand, and hoped like hell the shock wouldn't cause her to drop it.

"Mum," she said quickly, drawing her mother's attention, "I'm sorry I can't get up and say hello properly, but I've got a sprained ankle. Luke here has been looking after me. And, as you can see, he's kindly stepped in to do the cooking for us today, too. You remember Luke."

Victoria wandered over to the kitchen table, looking dazed, and, to Rosie's relief, put the bottle of wine down. Blinking at her daughter, she said, "Sprained ankle?" Then she twisted to peer towards the hob. "Luke? But he's in New York." She frowned.

"He's not, Mum." She took a deep breath. Might as well get it all out there. "He's living and working here again now. And we're... well... we're back together."

There was a moment of silence. Stephen, who'd been shifting his attention between the man on the other side of the room and his wife and daughter, shook the confusion from his face and replaced it with a big, beaming grin. "Luke! My boy!" He approached Luke, his hand stuck out to shake.

His relief obvious, Luke put down the wooden spoon he'd been using to stir something in a saucepan and took Stephen's hand. "Stephen. Great to see you again. It's been a long time. I hear you and Victoria haven't been well. I hope you're feeling better now."

As they released each other's hands, Stephen shrugged. "Fine, fine. Thanks for asking. Some nasty bug. I'm sure it's going around. We're not one hundred percent, but we're getting there, aren't we, love?" He smiled at his wife.

"Y…es," Victoria replied distractedly. Then she seemed to steel herself, before following her husband across the room and exchanging a hug and kiss with Luke. "Well, this is certainly a surprise! It's wonderful to see you, Luke. Handsome as ever, aren't you?"

Luke's cheeks coloured, but he smoothly replied, "And you don't look a day older than the last time I saw you."

"Pshaw! Still a flatterer, too." Victoria slapped his arm playfully, her own face flushing. She came over and took the chair next to Rosie's. "Anyway, I trust you two are going to fill me in on what I've *clearly* been missing."

"Of course," Rosie said. "Shall we chat over a drink? Dad, do you mind doing the honours? I'm sorry I'm not being a very good host, but…" she pointed in the direction of her ankle, which she'd carefully eased down from the chair her mother now sat in when they'd arrived.

Her dad smiled and headed for the cupboard containing the

glasses. "'Course I don't mind, love. I'm sorry you've hurt your ankle. So, what are we all having? Luke? I feel I should look after the chef first, since he's doing all the graft."

"A non-alcoholic beer from the fridge for me, please, Stephen," Luke said, opening the oven to check on everything. "I've got work this evening, so I can't drink much. I'll have a nice glass of wine with my dinner and that'll be my lot."

"No problem." Stephen pulled out a glass, then clapped the younger man fondly on the back on his way to the fridge. "Bit of a busman's holiday then, this. Cooking today, then tonight, too. Poor sod."

Luke grinned. "I don't mind. I wouldn't be doing the job I do if I didn't enjoy cooking. And besides, with Rosie temporarily incapacitated, what else was I going to do? You've already missed out on one Christmas Day—I don't want you to miss another one."

"It's very nice of you, love," Victoria said, flashing a sweet smile in Luke's direction, before turning to her daughter with a narrow-eyed look. "So, how did you hurt your ankle? Weren't you in the shop yesterday? You didn't tumble off that rickety bloody stepladder, did you? I'm always telling y—"

"No, Mum." Rosie shook her head exasperatedly. "It was nothing to do with the stepladder. I slipped in the car park behind the shop, that's all. On a manhole cover. Went down, twisted my ankle in the process. It's just a sprain. I've been icing it, elevating it, taking painkillers, all that. It already feels better than it did yesterday, and the swelling's gone down a bit. Luckily, Luke met me from work, so he was able to help me up, get me into the car and bring me home.

He's been an excellent nursemaid." Well, saying Luke met her from work wasn't a lie, was it? Just a convenient manipulation of the truth. Her parents didn't need to know the ins and outs of what had taken place over the last few days.

"What are you ladies having?" Stephen asked, having placed Luke's glass of beer within easy reach on the worksurface.

"I'll have one of those beers too, please, Dad. I don't want to drink too much either, because of the painkillers. I'll have wine with dinner, too. But help yourselves to whatever you want from the fridge or the wine rack. Oh, and I've also got gin, cream liqueur, sherry..." She glanced hopefully at her mother.

Victoria straightened. "Ooh, sherry. You know what, I'd love a sherry. This is our Christmas Day re-do, after all. Not quite the day I expected, mind." She glanced over at Luke, then back to her daughter, the look in her eyes accusatory.

Just then, Stephen came over with a glass holding Rosie's beer. He placed it down in front of her.

"Thanks, Dad. You're a star. Sherry's in the sideboard."

Her father smiled and ruffled her hair. "You're welcome, love. Table looks great, by the way."

Rosie had gone all out, decorating the table the same way she'd planned to do before their original Christmas Day plans went awry. A beautiful deep-red and gold patterned tablecloth sat beneath placemats in matching colours. Her nicest cutlery surrounded each place setting, and a stunning centrepiece featuring lots of seasonal greenery, as well as bright red holly berries and a poinsettia took pride of place. Topping it off, the luxury Christmas crackers she'd purchased what now felt like months ago, but was in reality only a couple of weeks. So much had happened in such a short space of time. She was happy—God, was she happy—but that didn't mean she wasn't still reeling.

"Thanks, Dad." She beamed at his retreating back before turning to see her mother still staring at her expectantly. *Bloody hell. Just rip the plaster off, Rosie. It'll hurt less.*

She glanced over at Luke, who'd stopped to take a sip of his beer. Their eyes met, and she raised a questioning eyebrow. He gave a barely perceptible nod in response.

Rosie took a deep breath and focused on her mother, wondering how best to word things. At least they were getting the conversation out of the way before dinner—not that Victoria knew, but some of it wasn't suitable mealtime chatter—so it could sink in and allow them to enjoy their food when it came.

She took a swig of her own beer, lamenting the fact it would give her precisely zero percent Dutch courage, then put the glass down and took her mother's hand. "Mum. I'm going to get the horrible bit out of the way first, okay?"

Victoria frowned and nodded unsteadily. "Okay… Should we wait for your dad?"

Stephen arrived at that moment, then placed the glass of sherry in front of his wife, before taking a seat with a glass of his own. "I'm here. What is it?" He glanced between his wife and daughter, his brow drawing low. "Is everything all right?"

She swallowed hard. "Not really. I'm sorry to have to let you know, but Luke's mum, Cathy, passed away a few months ago.

That's why he came back from New York." Peering in his direction, she saw Luke hunched very deliberately over the stove, probably hiding or holding back tears. Once again, she ached to go and give him a hug. She supposed technically she could, but by the time she got there, with all the drama that would entail, the moment would have passed. And besides, the quicker she got this part of the tale told, the sooner she could move on to the less depressing bits.

She turned back to her parents. Tears shimmered in Victoria's widened eyes, and Stephen's face had paled. They'd known Cathy, of course—though the two lots of parents didn't socialise without their children present—and had been on friendly terms, so it had to be a shock. "S-she… it was sudden. Luke and his dad were with her when it happened. I can tell you more… but maybe not today, eh? We should try to keep today about positive, happy things."

Stephen cleared his throat, ran a hand through his hair, then nodded. His voice came out a tad strangled as he said, "Y-yes, of course, love. No problem." He swallowed, then turned in Luke's direction. The man in question was still hunched intently over the hob, poking and prodding at the various things cooking on top of it. "I'm really sorry for your loss, Luke. She was a good woman, your mum."

"She was," Victoria added. "I'm sorry too, love. I'll always have fond memories of her."

Luke straightened, took a deep breath, then faced them—a watery smile on his face. "Thank you both. I appreciate it. But Rosie's right. Let's keep today about positive, happy things, shall we? Speaking of which, I'm ready to crack out the starters!"

"Stellar news," Stephen said, clapping his hands and rubbing them together excitedly. "Our Rosie's a fine cook, but it's not every day you get your Christmas dinner prepared by a professional chef, is it? I'm looking forward to this, lad. I'll get the wine." He got to his feet and bustled off.

Victoria took a large gulp of her sherry, then put the glass down with a slightly trembling hand, clearly trying to get a handle on the sad news—or at least pushing it down deep to deal with later. "D-do you need any help, Luke, love?"

"Stay right where you are," he commanded, whisking four plates of pâté out of the fridge and putting them down on the worksurface, where he added the bread and side salad. "Enjoy your sherry. I've got everything in hand. But thank you."

Victoria and Rosie exchanged an amused look. "Okay, love. Whatever you say."

Both men approached the table at the same time—Stephen with wine and a corkscrew, Luke with the starters. With some dodging and weaving, the two of them got everything where it needed to go, then Stephen took care of opening and pouring the wine as Luke did a quick check to make sure everything was okay with the main course, ditched his apron, then joined them at the table.

Eager to move on from the lingering sombre mood—for Luke's sake as much as anything—Rosie scooped up her glass of red wine and held it aloft. "Cheers, everyone, and Merry Christmas!"

The others joined in, and a series of clinking and swigging

followed. Then Rosie added, "Crackers, everyone. And I want hats *on*, please. Not a word about it ruining your hair, Mum. It's a paper hat, not a motorcycle helmet."

Victoria pulled a face at her daughter, then picked up her cracker. For the second time in less than a week, Rosie assumed the cracker-pulling position with those seated around a table with her. This time, she was the one to say, "Ready? One... two... three!"

Within minutes, the mood had lightened considerably. After all, who could be sad when wearing a daft paper hat and reading out and listening to corny cracker jokes? Even the playlist had joined in, belting out a cheery rendition of *Santa Claus is Coming to Town* by Bruce Springsteen and the E Street Band.

As the giggles petered out, Luke said, "Right then, you lot. Let's dig in, shall we? I don't want the main event to end up overcooked."

"Heaven forbid," Stephen said indignantly, snatching up his starter fork so quickly it set Rosie's giggles off again.

Unsurprisingly, with a pro at the helm, the meal went without a hitch. They ate and chatted and laughed, enjoying one another's company as well as the delicious food. The atmosphere was as warm and fuzzy as it was possible to be, absolutely perfect for a Christmas Day re-do. Once again, Rosie thought, it was as if the last decade had never happened.

"Blimey, lad," Stephen said, putting down his fork and sitting back heavily in his chair. "That was incredible. I'm more stuffed than that turkey we've just enjoyed." He placed his hands on his stomach with a satisfied smile.

Luke scooped up the last of the dessert on his own plate. "I'm glad you enjoyed it. I only hope my roulade was as good as Rosie's. I mean, it was her recipe, and she supervised, but I made it." He popped the laden fork in his mouth.

Stephen shifted uncomfortably in his chair, flicking his gaze between Luke and Rosie. "Er…"

"Don't answer that, Dad!" Rosie said with a chuckle, shaking her head. "There's no right answer." She smacked Luke's forearm. "Stop fishing for compliments, you. You're already a renowned chef with a bazillion five-star reviews to your name—what more do you want?"

He swallowed his last bite of roulade and put the fork down. "Actually," he replied, flashing her an enormous grin, "I'm glad you asked that question. Because there *is* something I'd like."

Rosie frowned. "What are you on about?"

He stood, still grinning, then reached into his jeans pocket and pulled something out. As her brain struggled to compute what was going on, Luke stepped around the table and went down on one knee in front of her. Victoria gasped. Rosie's heart began to race as the penny finally dropped.

"I'd actually like to ask a question, too," he said, flipping open the lid of the small velvet box to reveal a beautiful engagement ring with two smaller pink gemstones set on either side of a gleaming diamond. Nerves lacing his voice, he continued, "Rosie Kilbride. I was going to ask you this over ten years ago, with this very ring, but if the last few months have taught me anything, it's that it's better late than never. I love you. I never stopped. So… will you marry me?"

Before Rosie could formulate a response, given she was reeling with shock, the next song on the playlist faded in. Her mouth fell open as the infamous Mariah Carey lyrics reached her ears. This time, rather than being overwhelmed by unwelcome emotion, she let out a startled splutter of laughter. She stared at Luke, puzzled. "Did you..?"

He shook his head, looking a bit taken aback himself. "Not guilty. Just an absolutely bonkers coincidence. Or maybe it's a sign from the universe, telling you you should say yes." He wiggled his eyebrows suggestively.

"I don't need a sign from the universe, you bloody idiot." She leaned over and flung her arms around his neck. "Of *course* I'll marry you!"

As Luke lifted her from her chair and swung her around, her bad ankle entirely forgotten, Rosie felt lighter than air—in more ways than one. Four days ago, this scenario hadn't even featured in her wildest of cheese dreams. But with Luke back in her life, she could hardly imagine any other outcome—albeit one that was coming to fruition way more quickly than she'd expected. Given all the pieces of the jigsaw—both good *and* bad—that had had to slot into place to build this amazing picture, though, who was she to argue?

*****

A note from the author: Thank you so much for reading

When Christmas is Cancelled. If you enjoyed it, please do tell your friends, family, colleagues, book clubs, and so on. Also, posting a short review on the retailer site you bought the book from (as well as Goodreads and BookBub, if you have them) would be incredibly helpful and very much appreciated. There are lots of books out there, which makes word of mouth an author's best friend, and also allows us to keep doing what we love doing—writing.

About the Author

Lucy Felthouse is the award-winning author of erotic romance novels *Stately Pleasures* (named in the top 5 of Cliterati.co.uk's 100 Modern Erotic Classics That You've Never Heard Of), *Eyes Wide Open* (winner of the Love Romances Café's Best Ménage Book 2015 award), *The Persecution of the Wolves, Hiding in Plain Sight, Curve Appeal, Not That Kind of Witch* and *The Heiress's Harem* and *The Dreadnoughts* series. Including novels, short stories and novellas, she has over 175 publications to her name. Find out more about her and her writing at http://lucyfelthouse.co.uk/linktree

If You Enjoyed When Christmas is Cancelled

I hope you enjoyed reading *When Christmas is Cancelled* as much as I enjoyed writing it. If so, you may also like these other M/F contemporary romances. My full backlist is on **my website (https://lucyfelthouse.co.uk).**

Not That Kind of Witch

Can Willow let go of her fears and begin living her life again, or will her issues get the better of her?

Willow Green is having a hard time of it. Losing her job at the beginning of the pandemic and her elderly grandmother's 'clinically vulnerable' status have resulted in her becoming housebound. While her entrepreneurial, hard-working spirit and the knowledge passed down through generations of green witches in her family mean she has solved her employment problem, her fear of going out, of allowing the dreaded virus into the house she shares with her grandmother, is far from resolved. In fact, it seems worse than ever.

That is, until Joe Lane comes along. The handsome care worker turned delivery driver does Willow a favour, gaining her attention and reluctant admiration. He's got plenty of baggage of his own, but he also has the skills and temperament to help her with her problem—and he really seems to care.

The question is, will she let him get close enough to try?

More information and buy links:
https://books2read.com/ntkow

Hiding in Plain Sight

She had every intention of seducing him, but never expected to fall in love with him.

Mallory Scott is a British espionage operative—and a damn good one, at that. Her current assignment to bring down a group of diamond thieves and scammers should be a piece of cake. She plans to get her claws into one of the gang, infiltrate the group, and uncover the information she needs to catch and prosecute them. Luck is on her side, and within twenty-four hours she's lunching with Baxter Collinson, the youngest—and most handsome—diamond thief. What she's not expecting, however, is to get on with him quite so well. Attraction bubbles between them—and for once, on Mallory's part, it isn't an act. For the first time in her career, Mallory struggles with what she must do. Can she ignore her heart for the sake of the mission?

More information and buy links:
https://books2read.com/HIPS

Lottery Losers

Winning the lottery is a dream come true... isn't it?

Susie Parmenter and her husband of almost twenty years, Peter, are lottery jackpot winners. They've been able to do everything they've ever dreamed of—quit their jobs, design and build their perfect home, buy expensive cars, travel the world... So why is Susie bored out of her mind? She thought being a lady of leisure would be amazing, but unfortunately the reality is far from amazing. How can she possibly tell anyone that, though?

Climbing the walls, sinking deeper into irritation and misery, Susie can't see a way forward. But what she's not betting on is that Peter has noticed his beloved wife isn't happy. And he's taken steps—drastic steps—to turn things around. But will they live to tell the tale?

More information and buy links:

https://books2read.com/lotterylosers

And if you're still in a Christmassy/wintery mood, how about these?

Moonstone

Christmas gifts aren't the only surprises Ginny is going to get this year.

Moonstone Guinevere 'Ginny' Miles is in Silver Springs visiting her parents for the holidays. They moved to the town five years ago, and adore their new life here. Used to the hustle and bustle of London, England, Ginny isn't convinced at first—what's so great about a small town in Upstate New York, anyway? Despite her own opinions, it's clear to Ginny the move has done her parents the world of good—they look years younger. There's clearly something magical about this town.

Following some exploration of her own, Ginny discovers Silver Springs has its charms—Jewels Cafe is amazing, for starters, as is its pumpkin spice latte. Ginny's drunk a lot of lattes in her thirty-three years, but nothing quite like this.

Her taste buds are still tingling from the tasty treat when she comes across a broken-down truck on the way back to her parents' place. And when she spots the three gorgeous guys with the vehicle, it's not just her taste buds that are tingling.

Is Ginny's vacation in Silver Springs about to get a whole lot more interesting?

More information and buy links:
https://books2read.com/moonstoneJC

Cupid

What if Santa's reindeer were shifters?

As a postman by day, and one of Santa's reindeer on a single very special night, Cassius Cupid eats, sleeps, and breathes deliveries. He doesn't mind, but sometimes wishes that someone would send him something more exciting than bills and junk mail.

One cold January morning, Cassius gets his wish. A young woman arrives with a parcel. Turns out it's for his housemate – but Cassius doesn't care. All he's interested in is Carina, the beautiful female courier.

Has Cupid finally met his match?

More information and buy links:
https://books2read.com/cupidreindeer

Printed in Great Britain
by Amazon

53223805R00121